GOBSLAYER

KELLY HESS

GOBSLAYER

KELLY HESS

Cover Art by: Jeff Johnson – Johnsonverse.deviantart.com
Editor: Katrina M Randall – TurnThePageEditing.com

Print ISBN 978-1-988256-73-3

www.dragonmoonpress.com

A special THANK YOU to the Vacaville Town Square Writers for all of your encouragement and feedback on this book. You are a fantastic group of writers and an invaluable resource—Even those who claim Fantasy and Science Fiction aren't your thing. (*wink*)

FIGHT WITH FIRE

THE REIGN OF King Borlan was a bleak and unjust era for the Kingdom of Lorr, when those with magic abilities were persecuted and put to death on baseless accusations. On this evening, in southern Lorr, a boy and his father joined countless others to witness a popular event in the city of Shadow Glen.

Sitting on a ledge of stone, the boy gazed in awe around the White Arena, filled with thousands of restless spectators come to watch the latest of the Fire Trials. It was the boy's first time to the arena, and he shivered in anticipation of the spectacle to come. In the center of the battlefield below, large vertical poles had been erected, and three ragged souls, two women and a man, were tied to the stakes, each surrounded by a circle of piled sticks, brush, and branches. Barely conscious, the prisoners slumped against their restraints, either from exhaustion or starvation.

The boy turned to his father. "Can they really do magic?"

His father shrugged. "Who knows?"

The answer didn't sit well with the boy. Before a person is burned at the stake, he thought, surely someone should know for certain.

"I feel bad for them," he said. "What if they're innocent?"

His father gave him a sorrowful look. "They *are* innocent. There's nothing evil about magic, son." Then, with a sigh, he added, "It's just the way things are. The king fears magic, and the king makes the laws." He pointed toward the prisoners.

"These are the lucky ones. They at least have a chance. Most don't get the benefit of the Trials."

"It doesn't make any sense," the boy persisted. "How does the protectors' victory prove that the prisoners are innocent?"

His father shook his head. "It's just a show. The king created the Fire Trials to distract us from the injustice being done to magic users." He waved an arm, indicating the enormous crowd. "And clearly it's working."

The boy looked out at the throngs of spectators, all of them writhing for the event to begin. All of them enraptured by the thrill of the coming trials.

The Fire Trials. Spectacles such as this had become popular in the kingdom after some had decided that merely burning a person at the stake just wasn't exciting enough. In the trials, the accused magic users were guarded by a group of slave protectors as a horde of goblins tried to set them aflame. If the protectors could keep the goblins from lighting the fires, the prisoners would be deemed innocent and set free. If not, well, often the goblins were able to set the fires, but the protectors survived to fight another day, and sometimes the protectors were killed. Very rarely, the protectors managed to fight off the horde completely. Those who survived became famous, and their names were spoken throughout the kingdom.

A shiver ran down the boy's neck. He hated the goblins. The mechanized beasts were everywhere now, "keeping order" throughout the kingdom. Perhaps it was their lifeless eyes that disturbed him so. Or, it might have been their complete lack of compassion, or their frightening faces. Whatever it was, the boy feared them greatly, and he would root against them this day.

"Who will be their protectors?" the boy asked.

His father shook his head. "No one knows for sure. Not until they enter the arena."

The crowd roared as a gate finally opened on one side of the arena, and the boy stretched to see a man stride onto the battlefield. He was tall and dark, with a long braid of black hair down his back. For a weapon, he carried a spear with a savage steel tip.

A speaker, a fat man in a high seat shaded by awnings, stood and announced the protector's name. "Borodin!"

The crowd cheered and shouted the name, "Borodin! Borodin!"

"Borodin looks like a strong warrior," his father shouted in the boy's ear. "We're in for a treat today."

The crowd noise rose again as another entered the arena. Her armor shone in the scant sunlight and she carried two small swords, one in each hand. Before the speaker could announce her name, the crowd's chants changed to, "Larawin! Larawin!"

The boy looked at his father. "A woman?"

With a nod, his father told him, "Do not judge her by her gender. She is a great fighter, a favorite of the crowd. The only protector more loved than Larawin, is… "

The crowd errupted, drowning his father's words in a noise unlike any the boy had heard before. He slapped his hands to his ears and looked as another man entered the arena. He wasn't particularly large, but neither was he small. He wore black leather armor, and above his head he raised a plain sword.

The deafening sound slowly altered into a blaring chant.

"What are they saying?" the boy screamed at his father,

"It is his name: GolaStap," his father shouted back. "In the ancient tongue, it means Goblin Slayer."

The crowd settled as the three protectors took their places in front of the accused. The boy bounced with excitement. He'd heard stories of the Goblin Slayer. He'd survived for longer than a year, through many trials, which was unheard of for a protector. How fortunate he was to get to watch him in action.

Another gate swung wide, and the crowd noise sank to a hush. Preceded by the rhythmic din of their march, a mass of green-skinned creatures stomped in formation into the arena.

Each carried a short sword in one hand and a burning torch in the other. The flames of the torches cast eerie light upon their hideous faces. The boy gasped at the size of the horde.

"It's not fair," he said to his father. "There are too many."

His father nodded. "It is always so. Just watch," he said. "It's not as hopeless as you fear."

The protectors wasted no time. The three rushed forward before the goblins could gain any ground toward the prisoners. Before the boy could ascertain what was happening, four of the mechanical beasts went down. The protectors' strategy soon became clear: Pierce the goblins through the chest. The boy's father had explained before they arrived that the goblins, while mechanical, did have hearts. He had called them 'ractors' or something. Destroy the ractor, kill the beast.

The battle moved quickly and raged all across the arena. The protectors worked as a team, alternating positions on the field. Two of them would draw the bulk of the horde away, while the third remained protectively by the prisoners, fighting off any goblins that approached with their fire. Caught up in the excitement, the boy cheered loudly. GolaStap destroyed goblin after goblin, his skill with the sword an amazement to watch.

Things went well for a while, and soon goblin carcasses lay strewn about the arena. But, after bringing down a dozen or more goblins with his spear, Borodin became overwhelmed by a group of green-skins and took a sword point in his stomach. He went down with a yell, and the goblins around him turned and moved toward the prisoners. GolaStap adjusted his position to defend against the incoming beasts and Larawin retreated to his side to help.

The boy gripped his father's arm and studied GolaStap's every move. The famed protector parried a strike this way, then blocked a blow that way, then struck with a thrust. Dead goblin. But more and more kept coming and soon he found himself surrounded. He slashed and struck, spun and kicked.

An opening formed and GolaStap shifted for better position, but suddenly Larawin cried out for help as she too was nearly overcome by the masses. The boy clenched his teeth and held his breath. He could almost see what was coming.

GolaStap looked toward Larawin for a split second too long, and a goblin sword pierced his chest. A horrific gasp rose from the crowd as the great GolaStap fell to one knee, blood spilling to the ground around him.

"No!" the boy cried out. He covered his eyes to block away the horror as the goblins reached the condemned prisoners and lit the torturous fires. As the crowd went silent with shock, the boy looked. The goblins marched off the field, victorious. A group of armored men carried the bodies of GolaStap and Borodin away. A blue-garbed man walked beside GolaStap keeping a hand pressed over his wound. Larawin walked, head down, alongside him.

The boy buried his face in his father's chest and together they wept.

PART ONE

PLANS AND PREPARATIONS

ONE

A REMOTE REUNION

KALUM TINBROOK SLID the familiar sword into its scabbard. So long in his possession, the blade was as much a part of him now as his own heart. A technological dichotomy, GOBSlayer, so it was named, combined the brutal simplicity of melee combat with the high technology of modern genius. The juxtaposition of the hard cutting steel of the blade and the gamma disruption unit embedded on its hilt created a unique weapon with a unique purpose. Oddly, these contrasting elements of old and new, past and future, blended seamlessly as if meant as one.

The streets were black with rain. In fact, all of Millvale seemed mired in dreary shadows. This late at night, the shops were closed and the houses dark. The evening mizzle cast the streets in a blur of gray streaks. Standing in the road, he looked upon the only building that showed any evidence of life, The Lance & Barrel Tavern. Even from the street, he could hear the din of the crowd inside. He wondered if they'd come. It had been so long since they'd last met. A cold shiver trembled through him, and he pulled his cloak more tightly around his chilled body, ensuring the sword at his waist was well hidden. Normally, when meeting with friends he wouldn't carry a weapon, but this meeting had been arranged by an unknown, and that made him cautious. The odd choice of this out-of-the-way podunk village for the meeting only added to his nervousness. Checking the datalink on his wrist, he re-verified that this was indeed the time and place. He tugged his hood forward to hide his face and entered the tavern.

It had been years since Kalum had been to the L&B, but to his memory, it hadn't changed much: high beamed ceilings, sparsely lit tables, and the long and stout antique bar brought back fond memories of Kalum's time spent here. Adding to his nostalgia was the warmth of the fire in the wide wrought-iron brazier in the center of the room, as well as the cacophony of voices from the rough and rambunctious characters who occupied the smoky establishment.

New were the electric lamps that had replaced the torches that once adorned the walls, and the large display screen now mounted prominently in one corner. It brightly displayed some sort of battle between a female warrior with a sword and a trio of rodent-like kobolds.

Kalum instinctively scanned the tavern's inhabitants from the entrance and noticed a goblin standing in a dark corner at the back. One goblin wasn't much of a threat, but where there was one, there were surely others close by. Kalum wasn't surprised by its presence, though it was rare to come across just one by itself. The green-skinned beasts were stationed in numbers all over the kingdom. Taking note of the goblin's location, he made his way to the bar. The stale smell of old beer and unwashed bodies permeated the very woodwork.

The man pouring drinks behind the bar was even larger than he remembered, and Kalum leaned over and gaped at him. "Gods. Where do you find trousers that big?" he jested.

The giant slammed his fists on the counter and bent low, breathing heavily in Kalum's shadowed face. "You're very funny," he growled, "*and* very brave for someone smaller than my little sister."

Kalum grinned. "It's good to see you again, Gargan."

A deep-throated laugh rumbled inside the giant's chest as

he stood. "And you, Kalum." Lowering his voice, he told him, "Your friends are already downstairs."

"And the one we're meeting?"

The giant man shook his head and stepped away, but he returned seconds later with a large tankard of dark ale. He set the drink in front of Kalum. "That goblin over there is paying you a lot of attention," the giant told him quietly.

Kalum nodded, casting a momentary look in the goblin's direction. "I see it. Thanks for the drink. Do you still have a back entrance?"

Gargan smiled, his large teeth crooked and gray. "If I tell you, then we'll both know."

Kalum nodded again, took his drink, and made his way back to the front. With a side glance, he saw the goblin moving in the same direction. Damn. He'd hoped to avoid making a scene. Maybe there was still a way. Quickening his pace, Kalum exited the tavern, tossed the drink aside, and made a quick dash to the right, where he ducked around the corner. A steep flight of stone steps led down between the buildings into a recessed alleyway.

Pressing his back to the wall at the top of the steps, he waited, GOBSlayer in hand. Moments later there came the sound of heavy, evenly-synched footsteps. Just as the goblin turned the corner into the alley, Kalum struck, piercing his sword through the creature's chest. He felt the all too familiar jolt through his own chest as the sword discharged.

The goblin's glowing yellow eyes went dark before it ever registered Kalum's presence. Lucky. He withdrew the sword, the blade slick with whatever greasy concoction pumped through a goblin's body.

Gamma Operated Biomechs, or GOBlins, were robotic creations created by oppressive authorities to police and intimidate the living residents of the kingdom. A goblin's hardened-steel skeletal frame was controlled by a gammatronic brain, capable of communicating with other goblins. A small gamma reactor in its chest powered the creature, while the antennae implanted in their pointy ears and the transmitter that made up their long noses allowed every goblin within five miles to see and hear what any one of them chose to transmit. This made it important to take out a goblin quickly before it could broadcast or else one could soon be facing a goblin horde.

Kalum felt confident this goblin hadn't had time to transmit. Typically, a goblin's eyes turned red as it broadcasted. That hadn't happened with this one. GOBSlayer had been built specifically for these situations. The adapted gamma disruptor built into its pommel instantly fried a goblin's reactor and scrambled its brain if the blade made contact with any part of its metal skeleton, making it a handy tool these days.

The dead goblin teetered backward. Reaching quickly, Kalum grabbed the creature by one of its batwing ears and, using all of his strength, pulled it back and sent it tumbling down the steps, safely out of view. Goblins weren't very large, but gods, they were heavy. Looking about to make sure there were no watchers, Kalum descended the steps himself, purposely stomping on the creature's transmitting nose as he passed. Despite the darkness of the alley, he located the back entrance to the tavern and rapped three times upon the stout door.

After a few moments, a shrill, almost comically high voice answered from the other side, "Who is it?"

"If I tell you, then we'll both know," Kalum repeated the words that Gargan had passed him.

The sound of several locks being unbolted came before the door swung open. There stood Blemm, his oldest friend, his shoulders spanning the entire doorway. He looked much the same as Kalum remembered. He was a bit grayer at the temples and beard perhaps, but the twinkle in his fierce blue eyes still remained. Blemm was a warrior, through and through—tall, muscular, and born for battle.

"Kalum!" Blemm roared and took him in a bear hug. "It's

been a long time."

"Too long," Kalum grunted, disentangling himself from Blemm's embrace.

Blemm led Kalum into the rustic room beneath the tavern that Gargan made available to his friends. Unadorned rock walls supported a high-beamed ceiling, and the blaze in the oversized stone fireplace provided warmth and light. A heavily-built staircase at the back of the room led up to the tavern above. A long rustic table with seating for twelve served as the only items in the room besides the little man who lounged comfortably in one of the chairs. Hack sat up and smiled as Kalum entered. Dressed sharply in a fine suit, his fingers danced nervously on the tabletop.

"Hello, Kalum," he said.

"Hello, Hack. You look well."

Hack winked and checked his own suit as if to say, "I do, don't I?"

Kalum smiled. It had been long years since he'd seen either of these men. The two of them couldn't have been more different, aside from being his friends. More like brothers, Kalum amended his thought.

Blemm was a grizzled fighter, a relic of the days of non-tech. He abhorred technology and clung tightly to the old ways. Though he had conceded to wearing a datalink on his wrist to maintain contact with friends from afar, he'd defaced the leather band, carving it with ancient symbols of war and chaos. Kalum noticed Blemm's titanic war hammer resting in a corner, a monument to his warrior lifestyle.

Hack, in contrast, had enthusiastically embraced the new technology that had flooded into the world recently. As though born for it, his sharp mind was easily able to grasp the technical and detailed understanding of electronic gadgetry. Kalum had always known his diminutive friend was a genius, but it was nice to see that genius channeled to something other than his biting wit. And besides, technology played perfectly with his primary profession. He was a thief. Thanks to new and oft-confounding electronic ingenuity, Hack's success at acquiring belongings that didn't actually belong to him had skyrocketed.

"Where have you been hiding out for so long?" Hack asked.

"That's a long story for another time," Kalum replied, evading the question. The truth would only bring more questions that he wasn't ready to discuss yet.

"Well, now that you're here," Hack said, "perhaps you can enlighten us as to what this is all about."

Kalum shrugged and warmed his hands by the fire. "It's like I said in my message. An unknown party sent word they want to offer us an opportunity to make a lot of money."

"I already have a lot of money," Hack said. "Not that I couldn't use a lot more, but I don't like people who deal in shadows and don't make their identities known."

Blemm laughed. "Hack, you just described yourself exactly."

Hack winked. "You see my point, then."

"I don't particularly like it myself," Kalum said. "But any opportunity to get together with you scoundrels again is one I can't pass up."

"I fear it could be a goblin trap," Blemm said.

Kalum shook his head. "I don't think so. A goblin from the tavern followed me into the alley a moment ago. I think it was looking to question me. If there was a horde lying in wait, I don't think they'd raise my defenses by sending just one to follow me."

"Did it transmit?" asked Blemm

Kalum shook his head.

"Are you sure?" Hack asked. "Where is it now?"

"It's at the bottom of the steps outside, quite broken. It was dead before it knew I was there."

"GOBSlayer?" Hack's eyes lit up like two torches.

Kalum nodded. "Of course." He removed the weapon and took a seat beside the fireplace, leaning the sword beside him.

A giant smile stretched across Hack's little face. "Man, I love that sword. Best thing I ever built."

Blemm snorted. "An abomination if you ask me."

"Nobody asked you." Hack eyed the old warrior. "But my offer to make you one like it still stands."

"Not on your life. My hammer can disrupt a goblin's brain just fine, the old-fashioned way."

Hack shrugged. "If you say so. Your loss."

"If you're so enamored with it," Blemm said, "why haven't you built one for yourself?"

"We've been over this before," Hack replied. "I'm sadly too small to wield the size of blade needed for a gamma disruptor. Plus, a giant blade is far too unwieldy and conspicuous for my line of work. But thank you for bringing up such a sore subject."

Kalum put a hand to his face, hiding his grin. Just like the old days. These two couldn't agree on the time of day, they were always at odds with each other, but he had no doubt that either one of them would give his life for the other. Kalum realized that he himself was almost a bridge between them, a blend of the two. Like GOBSlayer, he maintained a balance of the old ways and the new. He didn't fear technology like Blemm, but he did hold consciously to the ways of old. And like Hack, he acknowledged the benefits of newfound gadgetry, hence the gamma disruption device on his sword and the datalink at his wrist, but not at the expense of the past. There was still nothing better than a good sword and a stout shield to handle any situation that came along.

He glanced admiringly at GOBSlayer resting at his side. Gamma disruption was nothing new in the kingdom, but it was typically only possible in the form of the latest blast weapons such as bombs or grenades. A high-intensity blast of dynamic micro-particulates was enough to disrupt the small gamma reactors used in biomechs. It was a technological solution to a technological problem, a way to fight fire with fire.

It was Hack who discovered the method of creating the same disruption using a conductive steel delivery system. For now, GOBSlayer was still, to their knowledge, a one-of a kind weapon, though Hack had warned Kalum to enjoy the uniqueness of the weapon while he could, promising to enrich himself in retirement by selling the technology to the masses.

Kalum smiled again. It was a wonderful feeling being reunited with his dear friends, like slipping into well-worn armor. A thousand memories of the old times flooded his mind. The old times, before everything changed. Before the Day of Arrival.

TWO

THE RHAST ARRIVAL

THE KINGDOM OF Lorr was everything it should have been. The stuff of legends and storybooks, the land was fruitful and the people were happy. Ruled by a king from a castle on a hill, Lorr had existed virtually unchanged for many centuries.

It was an autumn morning when the ships were first spotted on the horizon of the Infinite Sea. They were unlike any that had ever been seen before. Hulking and made of metal, yet swift and powered by neither wind nor oar, the vessels moved as if by magic. Nine ships made anchor off the western coast.

Those who came ashore brought weapons and equipment beyond wonder. They came not as conquerors but as explorers and traders. The people of Lorr's coastal villages met them in peace and learned much.

They called themselves the Rhast. They came from across the sea, from a land called Rhastor where society was driven by technology and science. They looked like men, but spoke an unknown language. Each wore a strange device around their neck that translated their words into the common language of Lorr, and in turn, the Lorreans' words were translated back. After centuries of mining, their land had been stripped of much-needed metals, and they came offering knowledge and technology in exchange for Lorr's natural resources.

News of the Rhast's arrival quickly spread and soon reached the ears of King Borlan, ruler of Lorr. Borlan, fearing the story of these newcomers' power was true, sent an army to the coast to engage them. It did not go well. The Rhast bore such a technological advantage, they easily put down the army's advance with weapons that fired bolts of energy and shields seemingly made of light. The Rhast were unbeatable. Or so it seemed.

Only Elbore, a magic wielder who traveled with the Lorrean army as an advisor, was able to match the power of this new technology. For magic was a force the Rhast had never encountered, nor believed to exist. However, no other magic users were present that day, and Elbore was unable to hold the Rhast indefinitely on his own. King Borlan had no choice but to meet with the newcomers and discuss an agreement of peaceful trade and cooperation. After a short deliberation, a deal was struck, and the Rhast boarded their ships and left.

Within weeks of the Rhast's exit, people's lands began to be seized by the kingdom. Taxes were raised and valuables confiscated. It didn't take long to realize what the king was after: metal. Any land found to contain even a meager vein of iron or any other metal was seized in the name of King Borlan. The Rhast ships returned regularly carrying new varieties of gadgets and gizmos, and then left again, their hulls filled with Lorrean ore. Soon, technology of almost every kind began to flood the kingdom. Even more than electronic gadgetry, the kingdom was inundated with other inventions such as automobiles and motorized horses called cycles. Paved roads and highways were built to support this new traffic. Long distance communication became popular with the introduction of comm devices that sent messages through the air. Giant data towers constructed throughout the kingdom carried information far and wide.

Along with changes to the landscape, the very way of life of every resident of Lorr was changed in fundamental and shocking ways. All from Rhast technology. Only the most advanced, cutting-edge energy weapons were withheld by the Rhast, for their own protection.

Around that same time, strict new laws were enacted banning

the use of magic. A booklet was distributed throughout the kingdom, supposedly written by Borlan himself, claiming that magic of any sort was the work of demons and its use was punishable by exile or death. Bounties were offered to anyone who captured a magic wielder, dead or alive. Fortune seekers and mercenaries took up the title of magic hunter and scoured the land in search of the demon-possessed.

Frightening accounts of people being burned at the stake based upon mere accusation sent terror through the land. The common people began to rebel, fighting and dispelling magic hunters wherever they were met. To quell an uprising, the king dispatched a Rhast-built army of mechanical soldiers called goblins to maintain order. Goblin numbers continued to increase until every town, village, and hamlet in the kingdom was under the "protection" of the king's minions. To make matters worse, in an attempt to seed excitement among his subjects, Borlan announced the creation of the Fire Trials, essentially turning the execution of accused magic users into a spectator sport.

That was ten years ago.

THREE

A PERILOUS PROPOSAL

KALUM SAT ALONE in his thoughts, the warmth of the fireplace relaxing his bones. He'd been away far too long. He remembered the life he'd lived before, his companions at his side. So many adventures they'd shared. Blemm sat in the far corner, re-wrapping the handle of his war hammer, humming an ancient tune, while Hack sat at the table hunched over a square glass plate, one of his many gadgets. His nimble fingers danced over the images and words displayed on the datapad.

Kalum shook his head in wonder. Everything seemed different now, but his companions were still with him. The years had separated them in time and place, but the bonds of friendship held them together for a lifetime. Just one message and they'd put their lives on hold to answer his call. And here they were, together again as if not a day had passed. Only one was absent.

He'd sent Trinn the same message as the others, but she had not responded, and he had not truly expected she would. None spoke of her, but he could tell her absence was felt by them all, an almost tangible void. Their reunion felt incomplete without her, like a puzzle missing a piece. He wondered where she was, what she was doing. Was she happy? Did she think about him the way he did her?

The door at the top of the stairs opened, bringing all of them to their feet. Blemm lifted his hammer in a defensive posture. At first it seemed no one was there, that the door had simply blown open. But then the curly head became visible, followed by a tiny person who stepped to the railing. She was a nobby, not even as tall as GOBSlayer's length. Her blond curls lay upon her shoulders like fog on the moors. She could have been a child but for her womanly curves, which she displayed proudly beneath a leather corset. "Which one of you is Kalum Tinbrook?" she demanded without a hint of shyness.

Kalum looked back at her. "I'm Kalum."

The nobby turned and nodded to the open door she'd just come through. A moment later, the last man that Kalum would have expected to see entered. He came slowly and deliberately down the stairs, the nobby at his heels. A damp green cloak trailed limply from his shoulders. His short hair and beard were now steely gray, and he walked with a slight limp that Kalum didn't remember. When he reached the bottom of the staircase, he stopped and looked at Kalum. The tiny woman rushed in front of him and stood defensively on guard. She eyed the three of them, her gloved hands resting on the handles of two small axes at her waist. Looking Blemm up and down, she flashed him a coy wink. Blemm cleared his throat uncomfortably, his face reddening.

"You look well, Kalum," the green-cloaked man said flatly.

"As do you, Baron Rothburn," Kalum said with a slight nod of his head. "How long has it been? Nine years?"

"Ten, if I remember correctly," Rothburn said.

There was a long silence. Hack looked at Kalum questioningly, mouthing silently the words, "Baron Rothburn?"

"I must admit," Kalum said, breaking the stillness, "I didn't expect I'd ever see you again, Charles."

Rothburn smiled but didn't respond. Instead, he turned to Blemm and extended a hand. "Charles Rothburn," he said, introducing himself, "Baron of Lenshire."

Blemm, still looking uncomfortable with the stares from the nobby, shook the baron's hand. "Blemm," he grunted.

"And I'm Katriana," the nobby rushed to Rothburn's side and held up a tiny hand to Blemm. "It's a pleasure I'm sure."

Blemm's red face deepened to scarlet as he gently shook the little woman's hand. Kalum couldn't help but grin as Katriana held firmly to one of Blemm's fingers, refusing to let go.

"Kat. Behave," Rothburn chided her.

"Fine," she pouted and released Blemm.

Hack made his introduction with a smile and a brief wave of his hand.

"That's Hack," Kalum said impatiently. "What's this about, Charles?"

The baron squared his shoulders with a heavy sigh. "It's Mariah," he said. "She's been taken."

Kalum stiffened. "What do you mean, taken? Taken by whom?"

Rothburn made his way to the table and sat, his shoulders slumped. "King Borlan. He's accused her of using magic and promises to punish her with fire."

"That's ridiculous," Kalum said. "Mariah has no magic abilities."

"Gods of justice!" Blemm cursed. "What treachery is this?"

"Of course she has no magic," Rothburn agreed. "Borlan is trying to strong-arm me into meeting his demands."

"What *are* his demands?" Blemm asked.

"He wants nothing less than my signing over to him all rights and deeds to Lenshire."

Hack coughed loudly at this. "That's some demand."

Rothburn nodded. "Indeed. Last year, we discovered a vein of iron larger than any that's ever before been seen. Borlan says if I don't comply in the next ten days and turn over Lenshire to him, he'll burn Mariah in the castle yard."

Hack rubbed the back of his neck. "Baron Rothburn, please understand. I sympathize with your plight, I truly do, but what help do you hope to gain from us?"

Rothburn looked at Kalum, an expression of pleading sincerity. "I want you to rescue Mariah. I know where he's holding her. I'll pay you whatever you want."

"Pshhht!" Hack scoffed. "Rescue her? From King Borlan?"

"Where is he holding her?" Kalum asked.

"Kalum, you can't be serious," Hack said. "We're talking about the Lorrean king here."

Rothburn ignored Hack's complaints and remained focused on Kalum. "She's locked in the top of Lorr Tower in Central City and being guarded around the clock."

"Oh, please." Hack put a hand over his eyes. "Lorr Tower?"

Kalum was calculating his chances. The odds were certainly not good, not by any stretch of the imagination, but it wasn't impossible. And this *was* Mariah they were talking about.

"There's one more thing," the baron said. "It is a Gold Dragon that guards her."

Hack shook his head in disbelief.

"Thanks for mentioning that," Kalum said sardonically.

It was no mystery why Rothburn had come to him for help, Kalum knew. There was nothing Kalum wouldn't do to help Mariah. But it couldn't be done with only the three of them.

"I'd need to enlist help," Kalum said. "A magic wielder."

"I know a few," Rothburn nodded.

Kalum shook his head. "No, I have someone in mind already." He crossed his arms and looked at Rothburn. "But I'd like to know, why us?"

The baron tilted his head. "What do you mean?"

"Surely there are others you could hire, those with greater numbers and greater resources."

"Simple," Rothburn said. "I know you, Kalum Tinbrook. I know your strength. I know your mind. But most of all, I know your heart. There's no one in the kingdom I'd trust more."

Kalum sighed. "And yet, that's not the opinion you had of me the last time we spoke, if you remember."

"I'm a father, Kalum," the baron said, his voice growing desperate. "I know I was rash and over-protective. You'd have done the same if it had been your daughter."

Kalum smiled. "I don't think so." He stood and paced the

floor, trying to absorb what the baron had told them. "I'll need a couple of days to decide, and then I'll give you an answer."

"Mariah's days are few, Kalum!"

Kalum shrugged. "I don't even know if we can do what you're asking. I need to do some research and work out a plan. If I don't think we can do it, you'll have to seek help elsewhere. Or else give the king what he wants."

"Think about what that would mean…"

"Think about your daughter! Is Lenshire worth her life?" Kalum shouted.

Tense silence followed.

"Okay, then," Hack said, rubbing his hands together. "Good meeting. I for one could use a drink. Anyone else?"

FOUR

A DIFFICULT DISCUSSION

Y OU CAN'T ACTUALLY be considering this," Hack said between swallows of ale. "A Gold Dragon? Are you kidding me?"

Kalum, Blemm, and Hack had bid farewell to Baron Rothburn and made their way up to the tavern to discuss the offer over a round of beer. The place had emptied quite a bit since earlier when Kalum had come in. Several tired-looking men still sat at the bar, and a number of what Kalum suspected were regulars, sat at tables in various stages of inebriation. A fellow not far from them was face-down drunk, sleeping off whatever he'd consumed. The large screen now displayed a scene that was familiar to any adventurer—a moonlit clearing within a dense and majestic forest. A crackling campfire burned in the middle of the expanse.

Kalum took a vast drink of ale and sighed. There were decisions to be made. The baron had left with the understanding that Kalum would contact him the following day with an answer to his offer. The nobby, Katriana, wouldn't leave before slipping a round data token with all of her contact information into Blemm's hand, giving him a knowing wink. "Call me," she had mouthed silently as she followed the baron out.

Blemm wiped foam from his mustache with his forearm and spoke quietly, twirling the small data token that Katriana had given him. He shook his head. "That halfling woman unnerved me."

"Don't be crude, Blemm," Hack chided the man. "She's a nobby, not a halfling."

"What difference does it make what I call her?" Blemm responded.

"It's demeaning. They don't see themselves as half of anything. You're three times her size, should she call you a tripling? She's a nobby."

"I meant no offense by it," Blemm said.

"Then why not use the proper term?"

Blemm grinned. "I didn't realize you were so sensitive to the matter."

Hack sighed. "I suppose growing up being constantly teased about my size has made me a bit defensive. I'm sorry."

Blemm dismissed Hack's apology and took another large gulp of ale, foaming his mustache once again. He scanned Katriana's token into his datalink, ignoring Hack's raised eyebrows. "Regardless," he said, "we cannot leave Lady Mariah to be wrongfully executed. It is an honorable quest."

"It's a suicide mission," Hack retorted.

Kalum stared into the brown ale in front of him, listening to his friends debate the problem that was tumbling around in his brain. He couldn't ignore the threat to Mariah's life, but the odds of the three, perhaps four of them, pulling off a rescue against a small army of biomechs and a Gold Dragon seemed insurmountable.

Kalum looked up to see another goblin enter the tavern. Blemm noticed it as well. "Do you think it found the mess you left?" the warrior grumbled.

Kalum shrugged. "I doubt it. It's probably investigating why one of their numbers went offline. Just ignore it."

Hack continued his list of objections to the quest. "Lorr Tower is technologically the most advanced structure in the kingdom."

"That's why we have you," Kalum answered shortly.

Lorr Tower had been built in the years following the Day of Arrival. One of Borlan's pet projects, the building was twenty-five stories of luxury living quarters on top of a giant gambling hall. A million electric lights made it quite a spectacle, and Lorreans travelled from miles around to try their chances at making a quick fortune. Few walked away enriched, but that never slowed business. Lorr Tower was easily King Borlan's greatest source of income.

Hack shook his head. "It would be easier breaking into the royal palace."

Kalum sighed wearily. Hack's objections were growing tiresome. Hack had always been the voice of caution within the group, never failing to express his pessimism of any job they took. In this case, however, Kalum was finding the little man's reservations annoying.

"This *is* King Borlan we're talking about," Hack continued. "The man can squash us like tiny bugs."

The goblin was at the bar now talking to Gargan. The giant was gesturing wildly with his hands and pointing toward the door.

"Borlan is a weakling," Blemm snorted. "He's nothing without the Rhast."

"That's true," Hack replied. "But in case you haven't noticed, he and the Rhast are quite chummy these days. There are hundreds of goblins protecting that tower. Kalum, we've always said there's no job we wouldn't do for the right price, but this is just crazy. Borlan is swimming in Rhast technology. Who knows what other kind of security he's got installed in Lorr Tower."

"That's exactly what we need to know," Kalum said, raising his voice. "Hack, I need you on this quest. We need to get all the information we can find on that building—floorplans, electrical schematics, security plans, key codes, everything! If you can't handle it, say so and I'll find someone else."

Hack sat back, his mouth open. He glanced sideways at the goblin, which had taken notice of Kalum's outburst.

Kalum clenched his teeth. He was stupid to draw attention. He knew he shouldn't be angry with Hack. Though the little man was always the first to point out the dangers of any mission, he had never backed away from a job. He could remember the old days, boasting that there was nothing he wouldn't do for the right price. How true that had been.

"Who else would you get?" Hack asked in a hurt tone. "Of course I can handle it. I'm just pointing out the obstacles."

"We *know* the obstacles," Kalum said, lowering his voice. "Let's just focus on how to overcome them, all right?"

Hack pulled out his datapad and began keying in requests for information, all the while mumbling under his breath, "...don't tell me what I can't handle. You want information? I'll get you enough information to stuff up your big—"

"You told Rothburn our need for a magic wielder," Blemm said to Kalum, as Hack buried his nose in his datapad. "I presume you were speaking of Trinn. Her presence is missed dearly."

Kalum nodded. "We'll need her if we're to face a Dragon. I'll have to convince her she's still with us. Problem is I don't know where she is, and I have no idea how to find her."

"That *is* a quandary," Blemm sighed. "The last I heard, she was lying low in Kale's Hollow. But that was some years ago." He looked up. "Uh oh. Here it comes."

The goblin walked heavily to their table, its lifeless glowing eyes staring. *<Is there some sort of problem here?>* it asked, its voice metallic and mechanical.

Hack was quick to respond. "Problem? PROBLEM?" He pointed a finger at Kalum. "Only if you think this man having a romantic relationship with his brother's wife is a problem. I for one find it repulsive and disgusting!" He turned toward the green creature. "But, what about you? You seem like a reasonable electrical appliance. What do you think of all this?"

The goblin stood silent, momentarily struggling to process Hack's words. Its yellow eyes blinked on and off rapidly. *<Physical altercations will not be tolerated,>* it stated finally. *<This is your only warning.>* The creature turned and walked away.

"Thank you, officer," Hack called after it, then immediately went back to work on his datapad.

Kalum shook his head, remembering their conversation. "Trinn left Kale's Hollow after a group of magic hunters took up residence nearby. It can't be easy for her, hiding what she is. I don't know where she went next."

"Did you send her the same message you sent us?" Hack said, not looking up from his screen.

"Of course I did, but she didn't respond."

"Did she read it?"

"Um," Kalum tapped the datalink on his wrist. "Yes. Yes, it says it was read."

Hack held out his hand, palm up. Understanding, Kalum slipped the device from his wrist and handed it to him.

Hack pulled a tiny retractable com-cable from his pad and plugged it into Kalum's datalink.

Kalum took another drink of ale and turned back to Blemm. "If we're going to reach Mariah in the tower," he said, "we're going to need a distraction, a big one. Can you take care of that?"

Blemm nodded. "I'll come up with something."

Hack unplugged Kalum's datalink and handed it back to him. "Trinn is in Terrawood," he told him. "At least she was when she read the message." He emptied the last dregs of ale from his cup. "Also, I can't find anything helpful on the local nets about Lorr Tower. But I was able to get the name and current location of the builder. He should have some information we can use."

"Good," Kalum straightened. "Tomorrow, I'll go to Terrawood to speak to Trinn. You two get whatever information you can gather on that tower. No detail is too small. We'll meet back here tomorrow night. Are we agreed?"

FIVE

THE TRIAL AT TERRAWOOD

TRINNITY MOONSHADOW SAT in the Gathering Hall with the other residents of Terrawood. She was in a back row, watching the proceedings. She had always enjoyed the circular chamber with its high arches and intricately carved wooden beams. But that was because the Gathering Hall was typically used for more pleasant occasions such as weddings, birth celebrations, or even town meetings. Now, an awful feeling of disgust grew in her stomach as she witnessed the cruelty and bigotry, stemmed from ignorance, that her neighbors were capable of.

In the center of the hall, looking frail and weak, Bethany Wilkins sat strapped to a wooden chair, accused of using magic. Standing over her, his white hair draped annoyingly in his face, John Skinner, the self-proclaimed master magic hunter, yelled accusations at the poor woman. Trinn's eyes narrowed in anger as Skinner described in a proud voice to the assembled audience how Wilkins had been starved and tortured for two days. Starvation not only served to draw a confession, but it also weakened the accused so they didn't have the strength to fight back with their supposed demon-given magic.

Skinner spoke grandiosely to the crowd. "Finally, after lying repeatedly for two days and nights about her knowingly taking company with demons and shades of unspeakable evil, young Bethany did confess to me that she has indeed conspired with dark forces for the purpose of acquiring magic powers. And she used those powers to cast sickness upon Gladys Miller, who, it is well known, Wilkins despises."

Bethany shook her head weakly.

Trinn cringed. The injustice was beyond reason. Bethany was no magic user. It was true the girl had been intrigued by the idea of magic, but she had no power in the art. And demons? Absurd. There were no such things; not that any of the people from this backwoods village could ever be convinced of that. Magic hunters were nothing but profiteers and scam artists, collecting bounties for capturing so-called magic users with no evidence at all and enriching themselves off the lives of innocents.

Trinn lowered her eyes as she called upon her power. *If it was demons they wanted…*

Skinner pointed a finger at the restrained woman. "Bethany Wilkins," he shouted, "I find you guilty of using magic and consorting with demons."

A haze began to form in the space behind Skinner, growing deeper, more distinct.

"You are hereby sentenced to death by fire."

Tears streamed from Bethany's eyes as her head dipped forward.

The assembled crowd erupted in cries of shock. Some cried out in objection to Skinner's sentencing, others in approval, but most of them cried out in fear of the emerging being appearing behind Skinner. The cloudy shape at last took substance, and the crowd went silent in terror. The creature before them was scaly and hideous. It had a man's face with horrifyingly exaggerated features, sharpened fangs inside a wide mouth, and large black eyes. Curved horns jutted from his forehead, and a long forked tail whipped behind him. It crouched behind the magic hunter, sneering grimly.

Skinner, finally realizing something was amiss, turned to see the creature. He screeched in horror, jumping backward. The creature pointed a clawed finger at him and spoke in a booming voice. "You've done well, John. Pleased am I with your service.

Your hands are stained with the blood of the innocent. You've held your end of our bargain, and you shall be rewarded."

Skinner was frozen in fear, his teeth chattering uncontrollably, his eyes wide in terror.

The demon turned on the crowd. "Sleep well, little sheep. With John's help, I'll have you all soon." And in a flash of fire, the creature vanished.

Trinn looked up to a pleasing sight. The crowd was running terrified from the chamber, save for a few men who worked to free Bethany Wilkins from her restraints. John Skinner, his face as white as his hair, stood drenched in sweat, gripping a table's edge to steady himself, and stared in Trinn's direction.

The sun shone brightly and Trinn squinted in its light after leaving the dim hall. Stunned villagers milled about, still clamoring about what they'd witnessed. Trinn made her way through the crowd and toward the cottage she'd stayed these past months. It was time to leave. Her time in Terrawood was over. Skinner knew it had been her; the look he'd given her left no doubt. He'd stop at nothing to capture her now. She had to run.

"Your illusions have improved," came a familiar voice.

She turned. "Kalum?" There was no mistaking him. His black hair was flecked now with silver, and the scar on his cheek was more pronounced, but otherwise it was the Kalum she'd last seen years ago.

"Aren't you concerned you're just reinforcing their superstitions?" he asked.

She grinned. "They believe it anyway. At least now maybe they won't be so quick to trust the hunters. And Bethany Wilkins will live."

Kalum nodded with a laugh. His face grew serious as he looked at her. "You look wonderful."

She tried not to react. "What are you doing here, Kalum?"

"We need you."

"We?"

"The group. Hack, Blemm… *I* need you, Trinn. We have a new quest."

Trinn shook her head and continued walking. "My questing days are done."

"Is that why you didn't respond to my message?" Kalum asked, walking beside her.

"Figured that out by yourself, did you?"

"Look, I know you're angry with me, but this is important."

"I'm not angry with you," she smiled. "In fact, I'd forgotten all about you. And it's not important to *me*."

"Borlan is going to burn Mariah for using magic."

Trinn stopped, her mouth open. "Mariah? What are you talking about?"

Trinn listened quietly as Kalum told her everything about their meeting with Baron Rothburn. He implored her to join the rescue, but he needn't have bothered. She'd already decided. She was going. Mariah had been like a sister, always kind, always encouraging. When Mariah and Kalum had gotten together, it was like having the family Trinn had never had—Mariah and her best friend. They were perfect for each other. But when Kalum so ruthlessly broke her heart, Trinn had sided with Mariah, and her friendship with Kalum eroded.

"I'll go, Kalum," she told him, "for Mariah."

"Gather your things and meet me at the road. I'm parked by the signpost."

"You're not still driving that machine, are you?"

Kalum grinned. Charming. Infuriating. "Of course."

She collected her few belongings in a satchel and left the cottage. Immediately after closing the door a hand gripped her shoulder. "Leaving so soon?" Skinner leered at her, an ugly grin on his face.

Trinn pulled away from him. "As a matter of fact…"

"Strange," Skinner said. "You didn't seem at all frightened

by the demon."

"I must have dozed off. Your performance bored me to sleep."

Skinner reached out and grabbed the pendant hanging from her neck. He pulled her closer. "I know this symbol," his grin widened. "It's forbidden, you know."

Trinn hit his arm away. "You're a fraud, Skinner. You're lucky I don't destroy you where you stand."

"And reveal what you truly are? A demon lover? Go ahead. Kill me," he dared her.

"I don't want to kill you, Skinner. I'm not a murderer. I don't believe you're truly evil. You're just ignorant."

"You're weak," he spat

"If you ever once captured a true magic wielder, you'd be dead before you knew what was happening."

"And yet, here we are. Alive and well."

Trinn stepped close and jabbed a finger in his chest. "Stay away from me, or I promise you, you'll burn." His eyes widened briefly with fear, and that made her happy. She turned and walked away, not looking back.

John Skinner watched her leave. He took a deep breath to calm his frazzled nerves. When she was out of sight, he took a small device from his pocket and switched it on, verifying that the small tracking tag he'd affixed to her pendant was working perfectly. Tucking the device back into his coat, he made his way out of the village, staying hidden. This town was useless to him now. He had bigger fish to fry.

SIX

MEETING MISTER HAX

A SLEEK BLACK MOTORCYCLE pulled into an empty lot in the downtown district of Queensland Bay. It carried two men and towed behind it a black trailer that matched the design of the bike. The rider, a small man dressed in black leather and a fiery orange helmet, parked the cycle near the road. The passenger, large and un-helmeted, jumped from the back as soon as the vehicle reached a full stop.

"That was insane," Blemm bellowed. "You will never get me on that thing again."

"Stop complaining," Hack said, removing his helmet. "It's just like riding a horse, only faster."

Blemm spit on the ground. "I think I swallowed a bug!"

"That's my fault," said Hack, unbolting a latch on the trailer. "I should have told you to keep your mouth shut while riding. All that complaining you were doing, I'm surprised a bird didn't fly into that maw. Now come help me with this equipment."

"Are you sure about this?" Blemm said, coming to Hack's side. "I mean, wouldn't it be easier to just beat the man until he gives us the plans?"

Hack shook his head. "You have no sense of tact, Blemm. You can't just attack people every time you want something. Take it from me, there are sneakier methods. Anyway, I've wanted to test this out for months."

"I miss the old days," Blemm sighed.

"So you've said."

Dirk Blackfoot keyed off the data console on his desk and rubbed his chin. All the information checked out. He'd spent the morning researching everything he could find about a company named Hax Enterprises. He'd received a message early that morning from a developer named Barnaby Hax. Mister Hax, owner of Hax Enterprises, was apparently in the early stages of building a new casino complex in Horn's Beach, a coastal vacation town in the southern kingdom. Hax had asked to meet with Dirk to discuss an offer to model his new building after the Lorr Tower, which Dirk himself had designed years before. When Dirk had informed Mister Hax that the plans were confidential, he had replied with a laugh, saying, "Meet with me and hear what I have to offer. Then decide how confidential your plans really are."

Dirk scratched his head anxiously and checked the time on his wrist. *Mister Hax should be here any minute.* As if on cue, a knock came at his door. "Yes?"

Miss Kornold, an elderly dwarf woman and his longtime receptionist, opened the door. "Mister Hax to see you, sir."

"Send him right in."

Dirk didn't know what he'd expected, but when the small man, wearing a yellow suit and top hat entered his office, he had to admit he was a bit surprised. Most unexpected was the silky black bird perched upon his shoulder.

Dirk stood. "Mister Hax," he greeted. "Good to meet you. Please come in."

Hax came stiffly inside and shook Dirk's hand firmly. Very firmly. "How about this weather?" Hax said.

Dirk smiled, rubbing the ache from his hand. "Yes, beautiful day, isn't it?"

"Yes." Hax took a seat in the chair opposite Dirk.

"I've done a bit of research," Dirk said, "and I must say, I'm impressed. Hax Enterprises looks like a marvelous business."

"Thank you," Hax said. "Now, about why I'm here. I want to buy the plans for the Lorr Tower to build a similar structure in Horn's Beach."

Dirk nodded uncomfortably. This Mr. Hax was definitely no-nonsense. Usually in his typical business dealings, Dirk liked to spend a little time with idle, yet meaningless, chit-chat and get to know who he was dealing with. But Hax was clearly not typical. Well, no matter.

"I see you're a man who likes to get straight to the meat," Dirk said. "You said in your message you had an offer of some kind."

"Yes," Hax said flatly. "Thirty-five thousand for all of your Lorr Tower plans."

Dirk coughed, choking on his own salivation. "My goodness. That's quite an offer."

Indeed, he'd not expected half that amount. Having recovered from his coughing fit, Dirk smiled his best smile, teeth and all. "That sounds reasonable."

The bird on Mister Hax's shoulder fluttered wildly, flying over the top of Dirk's head and landing on the bookshelf behind him.

"How about this weather?" Hax said.

Dirked frowned. There was something very odd about this Mister Hax. "Lovely."

"I'd like to see an example of the plans, if I may," Hax said. "A sample of the goods, before I buy, you understand."

Dirk couldn't put his finger on what it was about Mister Hax that bothered him. The man was blunt and short of words, but that wasn't it. Still, he could understand anyone requesting a sample before spending thirty-five thousand. *Thirty-five thousand! How nice that sounded.*

"Of course, Mister Hax," Dirk said, tapping his console to life. "It will take me just a moment to pull up the plans. I'll print out a basic floorplan of one of the floors, will that suffice?" He accessed the net and keyed in his password to reach the company records.

"That will be fine," Hax said, nodding.

They sat in silence as Dirk sent the drawing file to the printer. He watched Hax out of the corner of his eye. The man sat motionless in his seat, an odd grin on his face, staring at the back of the data console. He was completely motionless, like a statue. A bad feeling crept over Dirk. There was something very odd about this man, and it made him nervous. These plans technically belonged to King Borlan. But Dirk had no reason to suspect Mister Hax was up to misdeeds. He was a weird one that was for sure. But he was also a rich one. Still...

"How about this weather?" Hax said.

"No." Dirk clicked off the console. "I'm sorry, Mister Hax, but the plans are not for sale."

"I'm sorry to hear that." Hax stood, and the bird fluttered back onto his shoulder. "Have a nice day." The strange little man turned and left his office without another word.

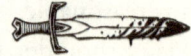

"Well that didn't work," Blemm said, watching the display on Hack's datapad. "All that talk about the weather scared him off."

Hack nodded. "Yeah. I'll need to do a little tweaking."

"So, now can we go beat him up?"

"Blemm, we don't need to beat him up. I have his password. I can access the plans whenever we want." He punched away at the pad for a moment. "There. Now they're all saved on here, just in case Blackfoot gets wise and changes his password."

"How did you get his password? His hands were hidden behind the console...." Blemm paused, realization dawning over his face. "The bird!"

Hack winked. "Bird's eye view." He opened the cover on the trailer. "He needs a little debugging, but I think overall, it was a successful test."

Behind him, a man in a yellow suit and top hat, with Hack's

identical features, walked up to them, a black bird on his shoulder. He went straight to the trailer and lay down upon it. The bird flew from his shoulder and landed on a small perch built into the interior.

"Why in Heaven would you build another you?" Blemm asked, a look of disgust on his face.

"I didn't," Hack replied. "The Rhast built it. I just modified it to look and sound like me."

"But…why?"

Shrugging, Hack said, "I enjoy my own company."

Hack smiled down at his latest toy, his own robotic doppelganger. "Nice job, Mister Hax," he complimented the robot.

As he closed the lid, the biomech inside smiled and called out, "How about this weather?"

SEVEN

A QUIET CONVERSATION

THE LANCE & Barrel was decidedly quieter that evening as Kalum sat with Trinn, waiting for Blemm and Hack to arrive. It was still early, and only two others occupied the tavern. Gargan stood hunched at his regular place wiping down a stack of mugs behind the bar, and a quiet old man, tattered and tipsy, sat alone with his beer at a nearby table.

For a while, they sat in silence, much like they had on their ride from Terrawood, where the only conversation had been him telling Trinn about Rothburn's offer. Trinn sipped a clear wine while Kalum nursed his usual dark ale. He studied her face, trying to determine whether or not she hated him.

"Why did you never contact me?" Trinn finally spoke.

Kalum shifted nervously. He'd hoped to avoid this conversation all together, but here it was. "I didn't think you wanted to hear from me."

Trinn shrugged. "You're probably right." Her mouth curled on one side. "I miss what we had, Kalum. I mean the friendship we had, before what happened."

Kalum felt his face flush and could only imagine how red it had become. Years before, the last time he'd been with Trinn, they'd shared an intimate night together, both of them overcome with somber emotions after ending other relationships. It had been a mistake, Kalum believed. He loved Trinn, but it had always been a bond of friendship. Now he looked at her, confused and conflicted in his feelings.

"I'm sorry." They spoke the words together.

Kalum frowned. "Why are you sorry?"

"Why are you?"

She looked so beautiful, and Kalum hated himself for thinking so. He cleared his throat. "I should never have…you know. After what happened with Mariah—"

"Which, by the way, I'm still angry about," Trinn said.

"I know. I was stupid."

"Why did you leave her, Kalum?" Trinn leaned forward. "Why did you leave any of us?"

His stomach tightened its knot. There was no way to explain. There was no good explanation. "Mariah was raised in a life of prosperity. A raggedy old treasure hunter like me could never have given her the life she's accustomed to."

"That's the baron talking," Trinn said. She gave him a sympathetic smile. "Do you regret it?"

"Every day." Kalum saw the change in Trinn's face. Her eyes lowered. Her lips tightened. She'd misunderstood. "I mean…" He sighed. "I regret the *way* I did things, not that I ended the relationship. She truly deserved better than me."

"You're too hard on yourself." Trinn narrowed her eyes at him. "You broke her heart, you know."

"I know." He'd always wondered how things might have turned out. He shook his head. "Anyway, the point is, I'm sorry I took advantage of you."

Trinn laughed, which was not what Kalum had been expecting.

"What's funny?"

"I just." Trinn stifled her laughter. "I was going to apologize for taking advantage of *you*."

"Oh, well then… wait, what?"

"Kalum, I never should have let it go as far as it did," Trinn explained. She ran a finger along the rim of her glass. "Mariah was like a sister. But, I was just so… I had always been…" She shook her head. "It was selfish of me."

"Have you spoken to her?" Kalum asked.

Trinn looked up. "Mariah? No. I was too ashamed. I wouldn't know what to say."

Kalum nodded. "I know what you mean."

"You won't believe this!" Hack appeared beside the table, having slipped into the tavern unnoticed, as was typical.

"Irwin, you scared the hell out of me!" Trinn admonished.

"Trinn!" Hack said, his voice quick. "Great to see you. And don't ever call me Irwin again." He gave her a friendly hug. Kalum grinned. He and Trinn were among the handful of people in the world who knew Hack's true name: Irwin Whizzlefritz.

Interestingly, most people who knew him assumed he'd taken the name, Hack, because of his keen abilities with technology and his less-than-honorable habit of hacking computer systems. But his friend had picked up the name years before the Rhast were ever heard of. When Irwin was a young and fledgling thief within the Thieves' Guild, he'd been given his first real mission, one of great importance, to enter the home of a wealthy landowner and steal a particular artifact, one of great value. Timing was critical, as the owner would only be away for an hour. Irwin arrived and spent most of the hour struggling in frustration to pick the lock, which was an expensive new one that he'd had little experience with. Finally, with time running out, he retrieved an axe from a woodpile on the side of the house and literally "hacked" his way inside. He successfully completed his mission and gained his reward, but he'd also gained an embarrassing new nickname among the other thieves of the Guild. It was fortuitous that he was able to alter his skillset, after the Day of Arrival, to better suit the name, Hack.

Hack took a seat at the table. "Now, look at this." He set his datapad where they could all see. It displayed a floorplan of one level of Lorr Tower. "There's a vault, a big one. It's right there in the underground level." He pointed to the screen. "Can you imagine the insane treasure that's in there? It's just sitting there, waiting to be stolen."

"Forget it." Kalum shook his head. He looked at the old man at the nearby tablet. He appeared to be snoring in his seat, his glass empty. "Keep your voice down," he said. "We're there to save Mariah, not loot the place."

"Yeah, I know, but Kalum, look," Hack implored. "I've done the research. I can get into that vault. Why not do both?"

"Rothburn will pay us all quite handsomely," Kalum said. "You can rob Lorr Tower another time. I need you focused on the rescue."

Hack put his arms up. "That's fine. Your loss. I'm just bringing options to the table."

"Hack, where's Blemm?" Trinn asked. "I thought he'd be with you."

Hack checked the time on his datalink. "He should be here shortly. He wouldn't come back with me on the cycle, so he bought a horse and is riding back." He shook his head. "That man is as stubborn as a dead mule when it comes to technology."

Trinn smiled. "But that's what I love about him. He's so completely true to himself."

"Yeah? Well, I'll bet his new horse is feeling every ounce of his true self," Hack said, grinning. "It's a long ride from Queensland Bay. And Blemm is no lightweight."

Kalum looked up just as the door to the tavern opened and two men entered. One was tall with white hair and wearing a gray robe. The other was shorter with dark hair and a mustache. He was wearing light-weight green armor. Kalum recognized the white-haired man instantly. "Oh, Hell."

EIGHT

A COSTLY CONFRONTATION

TRINN AND HACK turned and looked toward the door just as four goblins followed the two men inside. Each of them carried a short black stunstick in its hand.

"What's Skinner doing here?" Trinn said.

The white-haired man pointed in their direction and spoke to the goblins. "That's her."

"Who's Skinner?" Hack asked.

"Magic hunter," Kalum answered just as Trinn uttered, "Scumbag."

Kalum didn't know who the man was with Skinner, but he recognized his armor. This was going to be trouble. A contest of magic was surely coming. He hoped Trinn was ready for it.

The goblins marched in single file through the tavern to the table where the three of them sat. The first one looked at Trinn. *<You are under arrest for suspicion of using magic,>* came its mechanical voice. *<Come quietly.>*

Trinn stood and faced the goblin, staring into its glowing yellow eyes. "I'm not going with you anywhere."

Kalum and Hack stood, and Kalum positioned himself protectively just over Trinn's shoulder, GOBSlayer in hand at his side. Hack remained back, readying himself for a fight.

"Now hold onna shekkon," the raggedy man from the other table staggered to Trinn's other side. He leaned forward precariously on a walking stick and mumbled to the goblin.

"Yous has no right to bovver this woman." He shoved his hand in the goblin's face.

<*Physical altercations will not be tolerated,*> the goblin said, raising its stunstick toward Trinn.

On impulse, Kalum struck with his sword. He knew a jolt from a stunstick wasn't likely to be lethal, but he couldn't allow Trinn to be immobilized, not with Skinner and the other lying in wait. They couldn't hope to defeat them without Trinn's magic. The goblin he'd struck slumped forward on his sword and its eyes went dark.

Kalum pulled the sword free as Hack spun around Trinn with the agility of a cat and ducked beneath another stunstick that was thrust in his direction. A dagger that he'd produced from a hidden pocket appeared in his hand, and he jammed it into a goblin's leg, twisting and tearing with the blade. Hack had detailed knowledge of a goblin's inner workings, Kalum knew, and the little man severed the cable used to operate the goblin's leg. The green beast toppled over sideways and Kalum pierced it through the chest, GOBSlayer frying its gammatronic brain. Hack let his guard down for a split second too long to give Kalum a nod of thanks, and was jabbed in the ribs by another goblin. In a burst of energy from the stunstick, he flew backward, landing in an unconscious heap. Kalum winced, hoping his friend was okay. He'd hit the floor hard.

To Kalum's surprise, the drunken man sprang into the fight with unexpected swiftness, landing a solid kick to the nose of another goblin. The biomech staggered but came back quickly, its stick raised above its head. Kalum spun around and slashed at the goblin's exposed torso, knocking the creature off of its feet. The attack cut deep, and the creature fell lifeless to the floor.

Kalum turned, reorienting himself in the fight. Trinn had remained at a distance and was reciting an incantation for one of her most common spells: a fireball. A swirling orb of fiery plasma already hovered above her right shoulder, growing larger as she continued the incantation.

The last remaining goblin stood staring at her, motionless. Its eyes flickered between red and yellow. It was preparing to transmit a distress signal calling for help. Kalum shouted at Trinn, "It's going to broadcast!"

But Trinn just smiled, reacting calmly. "Here's to King Borlan," she said and held up her middle finger to the goblin just as its eyes flashed solid red. Kalum shook his head. She had guts, but the goblin's transmission was almost certainly going to bring a lot more of these creatures to the tavern soon. With a throwing motion, Trinn at last launched her fireball at the transmitting biomech. The flaming orb hit the creature in the chest and exploded, engulfing it in unnatural fire. The goblin twisted in place, its skin melting and blackening under the immense heat. Finally, it collapsed to the floor, destroyed, as the flames vanished.

"Skinner, you mangy rat!" Trinn screamed, wheeling around to face the man. "I've had enough of you." She pointed her finger at the white haired man, yelling out a short series of strange words. A line of white energy bolts, firing in rapid succession, thundered from her hand toward Skinner, who shut his eyes in anticipation of the impact. It was overkill, Kalum judged, for he had once seen a grown man blasted completely from his boots by just one of Trinn's magic bolts. But clearly, she realized what she was up against this time and wasn't taking any chances. Unfortunately, none of her missiles reached their target, but instead flashed and dispersed against a shimmering circular shield of light that emanated from the hands of the man in green, protecting them both.

Trinn didn't relent. Screaming in frustration, she increased the rate and intensity of the magic bolts. Sizzling blasts of light flashed across the tavern in a deafening stream. Tables and chairs exploded into splinters, destroyed by the deflected projectiles. Before long, the man in green stumbled slightly, seeming to weaken as his shield flickered under the magic barrage. Skinner's face took on a look of worry, and he turned and dashed out the door, leaving the other man alone behind his shield.

Out of the corner of his eye, Kalum barely noticed a towering shape barreling toward the man in green. It was Gargan, swinging his massive club. The giant's weapon roughly tore a gash in the high ceiling before slamming down hard upon the green-armored man, crushing him to the ground with a sickening crunch.

Trinn abandoned her spell and slumped to the floor, exhausted. The tavern was in shambles. A thick layer of smoke hung from the ceiling, and the floor was scorched and blackened from Trinn's destructive magic.

Kalum ran to Trinn, helping her to stand, bringing her arm over his shoulders. "Gargan, help Hack," he shouted.

The giant lumbered to the unconscious little man and, grabbing Kalum's half-empty mug of ale, threw the liquid into Hack's face. "Wake up!" he roared.

Hack sat up in an instant, blinking at the carnage of goblins around him. "What happened?" he asked.

"Stunned." Gargan replied, lifting Hack to his feet by the front of his shirt.

"Aw, I missed everything," Hack complained. Remembering to grab his datapad from the table, he made his way through the maze of dismantled machinery to the front of the tavern.

"Come on," Kalum said to Trinn, who still struggled to stand. "We have to go."

Trinn shook her head wearily. "I can't."

Kalum lifted her into his arms. "You can rest in the car. This place is going to be crawling with goblins soon." He looked up at Gargan. "I'm sorry for the damage, old friend."

The giant shook his massive head and waved him on. "I'll put it on your tab."

Kalum turned to the shabby man, who was leaning on his walking stick and watching them with curious interest. "Thank you for your help, stranger. We're in your debt."

The man nodded. "Elias Roble. Call me Eli."

"Well, Eli. For your own good, I'd recommend you get out of here."

Eli smiled. "I could use a ride."

Kalum examined the man. He was older; perhaps even older than Blemm, but his face had a youthful glow. His clothes were dirty and tattered, and the hands that gripped his stick, while calloused and stained, were strong. "Come along then."

Hack came beside them. "Is she going to be all right?" he asked, eyeing Trinn with concern.

"She'll recover," Kalum said. "She just needs some rest."

"What now?" Hack asked.

"Now, we go," Kalum grunted.

"What about Blemm?"

"We can't wait. Send him a message to meet us in Central City."

"Will do. See you soon." Hack was already tapping at his datapad as he rushed out the door.

NINE

AN ERRATIC EXIT

KALUM BUCKLED TRINN into the front seat of his car and keyed the button to lower the top. Some fresh air would do them all good. Eli fell into the backseat and strapped himself in, then quickly pulled a small tin flask from his clothes and took a snort. Kalum slid GOBSlayer into the scabbard specially built into the driver's door and fired up the engine. His car was a great black beast with four armored doors, shielded wheels, and a massive fray of spears and spikes jutting forward and backward.

The evening sky was aglow with the deep purple of sunset as he pulled from the lot. In front of them, a trio of approaching goblins was already blocking the way. He considered driving through them, but he quickly remembered the damage he'd once inflicted on his car trying to run over just one of them. The beasts were massively heavy and their steel frames unforgiving.

Looking in his rearview mirror, he sought the possibility of going the other way, back through Millvale, but he could see the shapes of numerous goblins, already coming out of the woodwork like cockroaches, swarming on the L&B. He had no choice. Revving the engine, he prepared to ram the goblins in front of him. He gave a quick tug at Trinn's seatbelt. "Hang on, honey."

A battle cry rose up from the distance. Peering ahead into the glow of the headlights, Kalum saw the dusty image of Blemm, charging on horseback, his war hammer raised above his head. Incredibly, the warrior took out two of the goblins as he passed with one mighty swing. The creatures careened to the side, battered by the force of the blow. As he approached the car, Blemm jumped from the horse and leapt into the backseat just as Kalum stomped on the accelerator, speeding recklessly around the remaining goblin.

"Where'd you come from?" Kalum said to Blemm once they'd sped safely away.

"I was only a mile out when I got Hack's message," Blemm answered. "Is that Trinn? What's happened to her?" Startled, he looked at the strange man sitting next to him. "Who's this?"

"Elias Roble. Call me Eli."

The two shook hands

Blemm introduced himself, then asked, "Where's Hack?"

In answer to his question, a black motorcycle, trailer in tow, sped past them and disappeared into the distance ahead.

Blemm blanched. "I hate that thing." With a glance behind him, he grumbled, "That horse cost me a fortune." Then leaning forward, he put a caring hand on Trinn's head.

"She just needs some rest," Kalum told him. "She overworked herself back there."

"She was wonderful," Eli said. "Dragons are no easy match."

"Dragon?" Blemm shouted. "Where was a Dragon?"

"A magic hunter came looking for Trinn," Kalum explained. "He brought a Jade Dragon with him."

The title of Dragon was bestowed upon those magic users who trained in the ancient art of Dragon magic, Kalum knew. Jade Dragons were among the less powerful within the Dragon Brotherhood, but defeating any Dragon was no small feat. Trained specifically in defensive magic, Jade and Sapphire Dragons were typically found in the company of more powerful members such as Iron or Silver Dragons, who were trained for magical attacks. Only Gold Dragons were masters of both offensive and defensive magic. Sanctioned by the king himself, Dragons were the only citizens of Lorr allowed by law to perform magic.

"Well, I'm happy you're all alive," Blemm laughed. "It's good to see each of you. Sorry I missed the fun."

Trinn slept soundly for a solid hour until the purple sky of sunset had darkened to the black of night. For nearly killing herself using magic, she was in surprisingly good spirits when she woke. "It's wonderful to see you, old man!" she said to Blemm in the backseat. "Your beard is coming in nicely," she teased. Blemm had worn the same beard since he was eleven years old. Kalum slowed the car and pushed the button raising the top so they could talk more easily.

"You look fine yourself, Lassie," Blemm told Trinn. "A bit older and more wrinkled perhaps, but a gentleman would never say so."

"Good thing you're no gentleman."

"Okay, knock it off, you two," Kalum said, smiling. He'd almost forgotten the good-natured ribbing those two always enjoyed. "We'll need to stop somewhere to recharge at some point, and I'll send a message to Rothburn, telling him we're going after Mariah. Eli," he said, glancing at the old man through his rearview mirror. "Is there someplace we can drop you? We're headed all the way to Central City."

Eli's eyes widened. "Well, then this is certainly a fortunate meeting. I have business in Central City. I'd appreciate coming along."

"So be it," Kalum replied.

The road ahead of them stretched long under the shine of headlights. The group was silent, each enveloped in their own thoughts and memories. Kalum's thoughts eventually turned to Mariah, his memories of her still vivid in his mind.

He was in love. The only true love Kalum had ever known. A baron's daughter, Lady Mariah enjoyed the finer luxuries of life in the kingdom, and she was well respected among the residents of Lenshire. Her relationship with the fortune seeker Kalum Tinbrook was only an embarrassment to her father. Kalum was gone for long stretches on quests and adventures and lived a traveler's life, which was unsavory in her father's eyes. He discouraged his daughter from the man. But, Mariah would not be swayed.

Kalum was a fine warrior and made a modest living as an adventurer for hire. But finding treasure was dangerous work, and Mariah worried dearly each time he left that it would be the last time. There came a day when Mariah took ill while Kalum was away, and a young healer named Jacoby was called to restore her. "It's the stress," Jacoby told the baron. "Her worries and fears eat at her stomach, and they will eventually kill her."

Mariah had always been interested in the art of healing, Kalum knew, and as the baron had later told him, she'd spent long hours talking with her healer about his work and methods. Jacoby waited on Mariah day and night, and his medicines and soothing potions did heal the lady. In time, he too fell in love with Mariah.

Upon his return, Kalum learned of Mariah's condition and was heartbroken to discover that he was the cause of her pain. The baron called him to his study one night and implored Kalum to leave Mariah forever.

"You are a good man, Kalum. I know this," the baron told him. "But, you are killing my daughter, and for that, I hate you."

Kalum had no response, for he knew the baron's words were true.

"A man," the baron said, "a healer, has asked for Mariah's hand in marriage. And I have given it. You must not interfere." He offered Kalum a sizable sum of gold to leave and never return. "If you love Mariah, which I know you do, you'll go."

Kalum knew he could never provide Mariah the life she deserved. And so, in misery, he accepted the baron's offer. Leaving her behind had been the hardest decision of his life.

TEN

THE SEEKERS OF
LOST GLORY

SHADOWS ON THE road ahead aroused Kalum from his bitter memories. He pressed the brake as the shapes took form. A group of goblins, maybe ten of them, walked in the road, one of them pulling a wooden cart. "Terrific," Kalum groaned. "More goblins."

The creatures stopped and looked back at them as the headlights washed over them. They wore crudely cut clothing instead of the leather armor normally worn by goblins.

"I'll handle this," Blemm said, opening his door.

"Blemm, there are too many," Kalum said, reaching for GOBSlayer.

"No," Blemm said firmly. "Stay here. Your sword won't be necessary." The big man got out, closed the door, and walked slowly toward the goblins.

"What does he think he's doing?" Kalum hit the steering wheel. "He can't fight that many goblins."

"I don't think he intends to fight them," Eli said. "His hammer is still sitting beside me."

Kalum turned. Sure enough, Blemm's great hammer rested firmly behind Trinn's seat.

The three watched from the car. As Blemm approached the group, the goblins drew swords and spears and quickly formed a circle around him. He was surrounded and unarmed. "This is ridiculous," Kalum grunted, reaching again for GOBSlayer.

Trinn put a hand on his arm. "No, look."

He looked again. Blemm was speaking to one of the creatures, gesturing wildly with his arms. All of the goblins lowered their weapons, listening to his words. Finally, the man bowed his head to them and the goblins moved as one to the side of the road. Blemm returned to the car and climbed into the backseat, buckling his seatbelt without a word. Then, looking up at the others as if nothing strange had taken place, he said, "We can go now."

"What did you say to them?" Kalum asked as he drove slowly past the watching goblins. The line of creatures looked at them, eyes wide with curiosity.

"What in the world did you tell them?" Kalum shouted, half laughing at the absurd situation.

"I told them who I am, and they told me who they are."

"Who they are? They're goblins, Blemm," Kalum said.

"Yes," Blemm said. "Real goblins. They are The Seekers of Lost Glory. That's what they call themselves. They're returning to their caves in the Atlas Mountains."

"Real goblins?" Trinn said. "I thought real goblins were extinct."

"Oh no," Blemm said. "They aren't extinct. After the biomechs came, they withdrew to the mountains, where they hide and await the day when the Rhast scourge is destroyed."

"Why did they withdraw?" Trinn asked.

"Because they're no match for the biomechs. When Borlan unleashed his robot army, it not only took control of the kingdom's people, but it also began killing real goblins in vast numbers. They tried to resist, but the biomechs' strength and resilience were too great."

"But why did they just let us go?" Kalum asked. "Goblins are usually quite vicious."

"Because I told them I'm travelling with Kalum Tinbrook."

Kalum stomped the brake and they skidded to a stop.

"What?" he shouted.

"You didn't know?" Blemm grinned. "You're very popular among the goblins. They know all about you and your mech-slaying sword. In fact, they even call you GolaStap."

"GolaStap?" Trinn asked.

"It's a name of honor," Eli said. "GolaStap was a great slayer of the biomech goblins. He fought and died in the Fire Trials. The name literally means, 'Goblin Slayer.'"

Trinn looked at Kalum. "Sounds appropriate."

Kalum just shook his head.

"How did you learn all this?" Eli asked Blemm.

"They told me."

"Blemm," Kalum said, exasperated. "That doesn't make any sense. Real goblins speak Goblish. How could you talk to them?"

Blemm shrugged. "I learned to speak Goblish a few years ago from a goblin I hired to work on my farm. His name was Glach, and he taught me his language. He was a good lad. Sadly, they told me Glach was killed recently in a mech raid."

"But you were only out there for a minute or two," Trinnn said. "How did you have time for so much conversation?"

Blemm grinned. "Goblish is very expressive. A single grunt or fart can speak volumes."

Trinn sat back in her seat with a quiet laugh. "You never cease to amaze me, old man."

PART TWO

CENTRAL CITY

ELEVEN

THE BOORISH KING BORLAN

BORLAN SILVERHAND III was a truly unpleasant person, which those who grow up knowing nothing but privilege and opulence often tend to become. Borlan's father, Silverhand II, was known for being a generally good man, but a terrible father. He paid little attention to his whiny brat of a son, except to provide him everything his meager heart desired. Young Borlan was never taught the virtues of empathy and compassion for other men, especially for those of a lower class, economically speaking.

Borlan had few friends, and he spent most of his childhood with the only person he ever truly envied: Elbore, the palace magician. Elbore had the power to do magic, real magic, and Borlan liked nothing better than to watch him perform spells such as making his white horse into a blue horse, or creating fire out of thin air, or little Borlan's absolute favorite: knocking people down with a simple wave of his hand. Borlan would follow the magician around the castle, pointing to random servants as they went. "Knock him down," and "knock her over," he would say. Even as a boy he was, after all, a truly unpleasant person.

Borlan never lost his fascination for magic. It was a rare power, even in Lorr, and he envied those who mastered the ability. Upon ascending the throne after his father's demise, Borlan, who still believed magic a learned skill, spent countless hours and great fortune training under the kingdom's most powerful sorcerers, but to no avail. He simply did not possess the essence, or aura, or whatever it was that gave one the power to do magic.

So, when the Rhast arrived and offered to trade with him scientific knowledge that could match the power of magic, proven by their ability to soundly dispatch his forces, Borlan was quickly seduced. In a desperate and hasty arrangement, the king offered a fortune in metals and mined ore, and he also gave them the rights to sell Rhast goods throughout the kingdom. If Borlan couldn't do magic himself, he would instead usher in a new age where technology ruled the day and magic was strictly outlawed.

It was precisely this new Rhast technology that carried Borlan now to the top floor of the Lorr Tower in Central City. Electrically-motorized lifts called elevators whisked workers and guests up and down the many floors of the tower, which at twenty-five stories, would be inconvenient at best with stairs. Elevators were just one of the new magic-like inventions that now allowed vertical expansion of such profitable businesses for Borlan.

But profits just weren't enough anymore to continue paying the Rhast. Iron had become scarce in the kingdom, for he'd purchased or confiscated as much as he could find. He'd even begun to offer them gold, a metal he had in abundance, but which proved to be less valuable to the Rhast as it was too soft a metal to be of great use. Borlan assured the Rhast that the kingdom was rich with iron and arranged to receive their technological treasure on credit while the ore was mined. But now, with iron sources nearly depleted, he was getting desperate, and the Rhast were growing impatient. Warnings had come that severe repercussions were imminent if a fair supply of the metal wasn't available soon.

Fortunately, a vast new iron deposit had recently been discovered in Lenshire, a prosperous community in the green district of Lorr. Borlan was determined to acquire this new cache of material in any way possible, but Baron Rothburn, the titleholder of Lenshire, was being stubborn. Borlan had considered sending a goblin army to simply confiscate the mine, but Lenshire was considered an historical gem within the kingdom, and the peasants in the area would likely revolt if Borlan were to deface the glen by marching on it. High taxes and goblin oppression had nearly stressed his kingdom to its breaking point already. A revolt against the monarchy was the last thing he needed.

And so, he'd decided to take a different approach.

A bell inside the elevator chimed as he reached the Penthouse level. The door slid quietly open and Borlan stepped out onto the landing, where a trio of goblins stood guard beside a set of tall double doors. A black-haired man wearing armor of gold stood motionless in one corner of the landing. He made no acknowledgement of Borlan's arrival, but his dark eyes followed the king's every move. To Borlan's annoyance, another man waited on the landing this morning. It was Mr. Freedling, his assistant and bookkeeper, who held a rolled parchment and a plain folder in his hands.

Freedling (Borlan had never bothered to learn his first name) was a tall man with a sharp-pointed nose and wire spectacles. The king found Freedling exceedingly boring and often made great efforts to avoid him, dodging down side passages, or even ducking behind furniture to hide from him. But Freedling would always manage to find him and then proceed to bore him to tears with mundane information about the goings-on in the kingdom and the king's daily schedule.

"Hello, Freedling," Borlan groaned. "How did you find me this time?"

"I keep telling you, sir," Freedling said in a nasally voice, holding up the parchment, "I keep your schedule. I always know where you are."

Borlan nodded, sighing heavily, "Yes, yes. Can we get on with it? I'm having breakfast with—"

"The decorators need you to choose the colors for the Card Tournament, Your Majesty."

"Yes, I know. I told you I'd do it."

Freedling looked at him over the top of his spectacles. "The tournament is in two days' time, Your Majesty. They need time to hang the decorations."

"I'll do it today."

"Please, remember this time."

"I said I'll do it!" Borlan clenched his fists in frustration.

Freedling unrolled the parchment with excruciating slowness and looked at it. "Oh yes. The goblin upgrades are ready. Puxley would like you to be witness to a test before he uploads. I scheduled you for after lunch."

"That's fine." Borlan's impatience rode on his voice.

"Yes, sir," Freedling replied and began rerolling the parchment. "Also, we've received news of an unfortunate incident in Millvale last night. A group of criminals attacked and destroyed a goblin team that was attempting to make an arrest on a magic user."

"Was anyone captured? Is there no one to interrogate?"

"No. I'm sorry, Your Majesty, but the entire team was destroyed."

Borlan stomped his foot impetuously. "Why didn't they call for help?"

"They did, sir. But the criminals escaped before backup could arrive. We did recover one image from a transmitting goblin just before it was incinerated." Freedling opened the folder he'd been holding and handed a photo to the king. The picture was of a woman, dark-haired and beautiful. She wore a mocking smile and was giving the transmitting goblin the middle finger as it transmitted. A bright orange ball seemed to hover above her shoulder. "What's this spot here?" Borlan asked, pointing to the fiery ball in the image.

"Magic, Your Majesty," Freedling answered. "It's the method she used to destroy the goblin. It was burned beyond repair."

"Have you shared this image?"

"Yes, sir. It has been distributed through all appropriate channels throughout the kingdom, as well as the goblin database."

The king sighed. "Fine. Is that all?"

"No, sir. The Rhast High Command sent another request to meet with you. This is their third request this week."

Borlan shook his head. The Rhast were growing more and more impatient. "I told you I don't want to talk to them. Put them off somehow."

"Yes, Your Majesty." Freedling pulled a pocket watch from his coat and checked the time. "Sir, you're late for your breakfast with the prisoner, Mariah."

Borlan's face reddened in anger. "I know that, idiot! *You're* the one making me late."

"Yes, Your Majesty," Freedling said and turned just as the elevator chimed again and the door slid open. A goblin mech wearing a ridiculous white chef's hat and an apron stepped out pushing a shiny gold serving cart. The cart was topped with several silver plate covers and two jeweled goblets. Breakfast had arrived. Freedling passed the goblin and entered the lift. "Remember the decorators," he called out as he palmed the scanner to close the door.

"I'll remember," Borlan mocked Freedling's nasally voice, "you twit."

He took a deep breath as he palmed the electronic sensor that unlocked the doors to the penthouse. He forced a pleasant smile and even nodded to the gold-armored man in the corner, who still had not moved in the slightest. The man just watched him without reaction. As he entered the penthouse, the goblin with the cart followed closely behind. Time to pour on the charm.

TWELVE

AN AWKWARD ARRIVAL

FOR BLEMM, THE ride to Central City passed quickly. He was surprised to find Eli to be one of the more fascinating people he'd met in a long time. The old man told him all about his life growing up on a farm in central Lorr. His father had been a farmer, as had his father before him and so on, back for generations. His family fully expected Eli to continue the family tradition, but he'd had other aspirations. He left home when he was only fifteen and journeyed north, determined to make a life of his own away from the farm. He had little money, and so he worked odd jobs where he could find them to get by.

Blemm listened, remembering his own childhood on his family farm. He recalled wishing, as Eli had, that he could break away and see the world to begin a life on the road. He admired the old man for doing what he'd not had the nerve to attempt. It was ironic that after all these years of adventuring and living his childhood dreams, Blemm desired nothing more than to return to his own farm, where his wife waited for him.

When Eli was seventeen, he found permanent work in Central City and managed to pay for an education at a prestigious academy. He married soon after, and within a few years his daughter was born. He worked hard to provide for his family and eventually settled down on the coast.

"Forgive me for asking," Blemm interrupted the man's story, "but that sounds to me like a fine life. How is it you came to be...?" He left the question awkwardly unfinished.

77

"How did I come to be this miserable drunk who now sits beside you?" Eli finished for him.

"No. No, of course not," Blemm stammered. "That's not the way I'd have put it."

Eli laughed. "It's all right. And it's true. I am but a reflection of the man I once was. You see, my friend, tragedy took my family away from me, and I have never recovered from their loss."

Kalum listened intently from the front seat, enthralled by Eli's storytelling as much as Blemm seemed to be. Trinn slept soundly in the seat next to him. He adjusted his mirror to better see the old man. He saw that his eyes were wet with tears.

Kalum yawned, his fatigue growing after a sleepless night of driving. Central City grew on the horizon as they came over the pass that crossed the Atlas Mountains. Craggy peaks towered high on either side of the winding road casting early morning shadows over the landscape. The great city lay before them, rising up from the valley with tall buildings and towers that reached the sky. The morning sun cast a heavenly glow on the amazing structures, especially Lorr Tower, which rose above all others.

"I ran away from anything that reminded me of my family," Eli continued, "which is to say, I left everything behind. I found solace only in the loving arms of strong ale, and I embraced it passionately." He sighed deeply. "So, yes, I am a miserable drunk." He lifted his chin and sniffed loudly. "But it numbs my pain, so there it is."

Eli reached forward and put a hand on Kalum's shoulder. "Cherish every moment you have together," he said. In the mirror, Kalum could see Eli's eyes move to Trinn. "It can all end in a brutal second." He sat back in his seat and turned to gaze silently toward the approaching glow of the city.

Kalum nodded, not knowing how to reply. Eli obviously had the wrong impression of Kalum's relationship with Trinn. He looked at her sleeping there. She looked angelic in the morning light. On an impulse, he reached over and gently touched her hand. Her eyes opened.

"You're awake," he said.

She nodded and smiled. "Yes, just listening." She turned in her seat and spoke to the old man. "I've not heard of many schools in Northern Lorr. Where did you attend academy?"

"Oh, I doubt you've heard of it," Eli chuckled, wiping a hand across his eyes. "It wasn't very well-known. It was called the Hall of Sacred Knowledge, but it's gone now, too. Just like everything else."

Trinn nodded and the car fell silent again. Kalum lowered the top on the car as they drove into the city. He still had a sorrowful lump in his stomach after hearing the old man's story. He wished he could express his sympathy, but there were no words. They drove down avenues lined with tall buildings smothered in lights of every color. They passed along the edge of a deep-cut crater of a construction site next to the Lorr Tower property, and then before they knew it, they had arrived.

"Gods of Light," Blemm gasped, craning his neck to look up at the tower as Kalum parked the car. "Nothing subtle about that, is there?" Indeed, the white building shone in the sunlight as if it was polished marble. Giant letters of gold, lit by hundreds of sparkling lights, spelled the words LORR TOWER across the entire top three floors.

"Wow," Trinn said, looking awestruck at the building. "That's amazing."

"That's horrendous," Blemm retorted. "What a godawful display of wealth in a kingdom mired in taxes." He stood in the open backseat of the car and stretched his arms wide. "Look at this," he said with disgust. "An entire lot just for cars. Does no one travel on horseback anymore?"

"The world has gotten ahead of you, old man," Trinn said.

"That's fine," Blemm replied. "It can go."

"I thank you for the ride, young fellow." Eli shook Kalum's hand after they'd all gotten out of the car. "I hope your goblin troubles are far behind you."

"Somehow, I doubt that," Kalum said, grinning. "Will you be all right here? What I mean is, do you have someplace to go?"

"I have friends close by. Don't you worry about old Eli." With a wink, he turned and walked away.

Kalum checked his datalink and turned to the others. "Hack is in room 1406." He looked at Trinn. "He suggests you disguise yourself since your photo from last evening has been distributed throughout the kingdom."

Trinn nodded and Kalum turned again to watch Eli make his way slowly through the parking lot. "Interesting old man," he said to no one in particular.

"More interesting than you think," Trinn said, coming up beside him. "The Hall of Sacred Knowledge was a school of magic—powerful magic."

THIRTEEN

MORNING MEALS WITH MARIAH

MARIAH SAT ON the edge of the sofa in the top floor penthouse of Lorr Tower and looked out upon the vast horizon. From this height, the ugliness of the city fell away quickly, giving way to the glorious landscape of the Atlas Mountains beyond. She wrung her hands nervously. Her mind was anywhere but on the view.

A small blackbird sat perched on the safety rail of the balcony looking at her. She tapped the glass door gently in greeting. The door was locked, preventing her from enjoying the balcony herself, but she cherished her quiet mornings, admiring the mountain view.

Eight days she'd now spent in this prison. Grand and luxurious as it was, it was still a prison, and she was beginning to wonder what her father was doing to free her. Borlan had shown her enough respect to not lie to her about why she was being held. Although the official reason was that she was an accused magic user, he'd made it clear that it was Lenshire he was after, specifically the iron deposit recently discovered there.

Oddly, Borlan had joined her in the penthouse every morning for breakfast. The king did his best to be charming and respectful, but he very often just couldn't help being a petulant ass. He tried hard to get any information or clues from her as to how to convince her father to peacefully surrender his land, but

Mariah had no answers to give him. She had suggested on day two, honestly trying to resolve the situation, that Borlan simply pay her father in gold a fair price for the iron. But Borlan told her that any offers of payment were met with flat out rejection by the baron. Mariah understood. Her father was a staunch opponent to the king's willingness to rape the kingdom of natural resources for his own obsession with Rhast technology.

But what other solutions were there? Borlan had admitted he would not attempt to take the land by force for fear of inciting a revolution. And now, with each passing day, the king grew more and more agitated that his latest scheme, that being to threaten Mariah's life, was not working either.

Mariah herself had to admit that her father's unwillingness to bargain for her life was puzzling. What was the old man up to? Surely, he didn't intend to just let her be burned at the stake. Was he planning a rescue? Was he trying to wait out the king, gambling that he wouldn't follow through on his threats?

Either way, Mariah's patience had run thin. If she were going to get out of this mess, she was going to have to do it herself. Her plans were well underway.

It had been clear from the beginning that Borlan held a peculiar affection for Mariah. He was never abusive nor unkind, save for her incarceration. She was being held in the largest, most luxurious suite in the tower, one which she would have normally paid a great sum to have stayed. She'd surmised early on that the penthouse was usually Borlan's own living quarters when he stayed at the tower. He was generous in granting her anything that she desired, outside of being released of course: meals, flowers, and clothing, all to her specifications. And on top of everything, his determination to breakfast with her each morning, which he truly seemed to look forward to, showed that he at least enjoyed her company.

It was this admiration that was the key to Mariah's plan for escape. On her first night, she had slept fitfully, frightened and confused by her imprisonment. The next morning, Borlan, showing concern for her rest, offered her a pill to help her sleep. "The day-to-day responsibilities of being the king tend to wear on me," he'd told her. "I toss and turn with worry unless I take one of these sleepy pills before bed."

Mariah had thanked him and put the pill by her bedside. But she was not so naïve as to willingly take a drug offered to her by her imprisoner. Instead, she hid the pill in a small drawer and began developing a plan. Having a scheme to escape comforted Mariah and she slept well the next night, even without medication. But every morning since, Borlan had graciously offered her another sleepy pill. Now she had eight pills in all.

Mariah looked up, hearing the familiar sound of the front door opening. Right on schedule, breakfast had arrived.

King Borlan entered the penthouse like he owned the place, which technically, he did. A goblin wearing a chef's hat followed behind the king pushing the breakfast cart. The smell of breakfast carried through the room and Mariah realized how hungry she was. Borlan greeted her in the same way he always did. "Good morning, Mariah. I hope you're enjoying your stay."

Mariah shrugged. "Could be worse, I suppose."

Borlan frowned. "Is there anything I can do to make your stay more pleasant?" He fished a tiny pill from his pocket. "How are you sleeping?"

"Sleep is no longer the problem," she said. "It's the waking hours. I'm just so bored." She went to him and accepted the sleepy pill with a smile.

"I'm sorry for the delay," Borlan said, "but your father is unresponsive. If we could just put our heads together and figure out how to get him to cooperate, this whole unpleasant business can be over."

Mariah nodded. The king was in a generous mood this morning, wanting to make her happy. That was good. He was rarely sour, at least not when he came to visit her, but there had been times when he'd seemed distracted, uncaring, or just plain mean.

"I just need something different," she complained, carefully plotting her words, steering the conversation. "I know you're doing everything you can to make me happy, Your Majesty, but I'm not happy."

"That makes me sad," Borlan said. "What can I do?"

Borlan had mentioned on previous visits of having grown up a bored and unhappy child. She knew that the best way to get him to respond the way she wanted was to be bored and unhappy herself. Mariah looked at the goblin that was preparing their meals. "I need to laugh," she said. "You there," she called to the goblin. "Do something funny."

The goblin ignored her, as Mariah had expected it would. She sighed dramatically. "Why doesn't it listen to me?"

Borlan smiled at her. "Goblin-82, sing a song."

The goblin looked up from the food and began singing.

<Goblins of yore, forever more,
Doomed to hide in fright;
Goblins of Lorr, forever more,
Destined to rule the night.>

Mariah smiled. "Did it make that up?"

Borlan nodded. "It sure did. Wasn't the greatest song, but it brought a smile to your face, and that makes me happy."

"GOB-82," Mariah said to the goblin. "I liked your song. Now, dance for me."

The goblin stared back at her motionless and Mariah's face turned to a devastating frown.

"I'm sorry, Mariah," Borlan said. "But he's not to obey anyone but myself. I can make him dance for you." He turned to the goblin. "GOB-82—"

"No," Mariah pouted. "Nevermind."

Borlan looked at her sadly. "Tell you what," he turned again to the goblin. "GOB-82, you will obey any commands from Mariah, unless I override them."

The goblin returned a curt nod. Borlan turned back to Mariah. "Go ahead. You can tell him to do something now."

Mariah's lips curled slightly. "Goblin," she said. "Dance."

In a thunderous jig that Mariah feared would collapse the floor, the goblin began dancing and hopping about. Every footfall shook the room; a picture fell from a wall, and the dishes on the breakfast cart tinkled and clanked. Mariah burst out in real laughter, for it was the most ridiculous thing she'd ever seen.

Borlan was clearly happy to see Mariah's mood improve. With a wide grin, he ordered the goblin to stop dancing and to carry on with serving breakfast. Mariah took a seat with the king at a small table by the balcony slider and ate her meal with the king over quiet conversation about her father.

Step one of her plan had been a complete success.

FOURTEEN

UNFORTUNATELY, FOURTEEN

HACK HOVERED OVER a computer console at the small desk in one of Lorr Tower's many suites. He'd already managed to break into and study the tower's network. He'd also gained access to the banks of cameras that swarmed the complex. He was able to display the view from any camera he wanted, but he still couldn't actually control them. That would take more work. In addition, he was able to access the hotel's schedule database and data archive. Since the cameras recorded everything and stored the footage to an archive, it was a snap for Hack to simply delete whatever video he didn't want to be seen later by the wrong eyes.

A message displayed on his monitor from Kalum. They had arrived and were coming up. Hack closed down the view of the vault in the basement he'd been studying and pulled up the data archive. In his exploration of the network, he'd discovered that only certain cameras were actively monitored at any given time by the tower's security team, so he wasn't too worried that anyone would see them coming in. But still he watched them as they entered the building and immediately deleted the footage of the group's trek to the elevators and their ascent to the fourteenth floor. Should anyone go back and check the records, there would be no evidence of their arrival.

Hack rose and went to the door just before they knocked.

He opened the door and invited in Kalum, Blemm, and an attractive blond woman he didn't recognize. "Welcome to paradise," he said as they entered. In truth, the suite was anything but paradise. The walls had been stripped of paint, and the beds, one in each bedroom, were pulled haphazardly to the middle of the rooms.

"We're lucky to be here at all," Blemm grumbled. "That confounded elevate machine is a death trap for sure. Imagine being stuck inside a box, hanging from a string."

"Well, get used to it, because this tower has no stairs," Hack replied.

Blemm looked horrified. "But what if it breaks?"

Hack shrugged. "It seems Borlan's obsession with technology wouldn't allow him to build something as primitive as stairs."

Kalum was exploring the ramshackle suite. "I like what you've done to the place," he joked.

"It wasn't me," Hack said, closing the door behind them. "The entire floor is undergoing a remodel."

"Getting frugal in your old age?" Blemm said, eyeing the disheveled state of things. A single painting, a portrait of King Borlan, was the only décor that remained in the suite. "I assume you got a discount?" He looked at the large window at the back of the room. "You couldn't even get us a room with a balcony?"

"Actually," Hack grinned, "I'm checked in to a lovely room on the seventeenth floor, one with a large balcony. But when I saw that this floor was undergoing construction, I chose to relocate here. This room isn't scheduled for work until next week." He sat back in his chair at the desk. "We should have complete privacy, but if we *are* noticed and they start going room to room looking for us, they'll likely skip the fourteenth floor all together."

Kalum nodded approvingly. "Good thinking."

Hack smiled. "Everything here seems to work: network, phone, toilet. It just doesn't look very pretty." He turned to the blonde woman. "Speaking of pretty, I don't think we've met."

The blonde put her hands on her hips. "You don't remember

me? That really hurts." And with a quick wave of her hand over her face, the illusion vanished and Trinn's familiar face appeared.

Hack laughed. "Fantastic. It's good to see you again, Trinn. You've become quite popular after your little stunt at the tavern. The entire kingdom knows your face. I trust you'll be on your best behavior from now on."

Trinn shrugged. "We'll just have to see, won't we?"

"So, what do you know?" Kalum asked Hack, taking a seat on the edge of the sofa.

Hack took a deep breath. "Well, there are over five hundred cameras, not to mention more than two hundred goblins on the premises. The cameras are set on an automatic priority algorithm, so only the twenty or so most important are ever actively monitored. And with the card tournament coming up, most of those will be focused on the gambling hall. So far, I can only see what the cameras see, but I can't control them or take them offline yet. For that, I'll need to install a jumper on the security server, but that's in another building, one that's being protected by three separate cameras and a palm scanner, which are almost certainly being monitored. Until I figure out a way to get in there, I can't do much with the cameras except watch. There are no cameras in the penthouse, except one that faces the elevator on that level.

"The elevator cameras are also on a separate network. So until I can install the jumper, we're blind inside the lifts. But since I have access to the archives, I can delete whatever footage I want."

"I noticed in the elevator we came up in there's no button to reach the penthouse level," Kalum said. "How are we supposed to get up there?"

Hack nodded. "Yeah, I noticed that as well. There have apparently been some modifications from the original building plans. There must be a secondary shaft someplace, but I haven't found it yet."

"They also forgot a button for the thirteenth floor," Blemm added, chuckling.

Hack shook his head. "They didn't forget. Early on, some of the more superstitious guests complained that they had no luck in the gambling hall because they were staying on the thirteenth floor. To avoid further complaints, Borlan ordered the floors be renumbered, skipping the thirteenth all together."

Blemm nodded. "Makes sense. Thirteen *is* a cursed number." Then he choked. "Wait. That means the fourteenth floor is really the thirteenth. Which floor are we on again?"

Hack grinned. "Unfortunately, fourteen."

That's bad luck," Blemm stammered. "I don't like this. Not one bit."

Hack shook his head. "Settle down. Thirteen is just another number." He turned to Kalum. "Anyway, I'm able to access the schedules of all tower personnel, including the king's daily schedule. Borlan is staying in the tower throughout the tournament, so that's something else to be cautious of." Hack turned to the computer, punched a key, and a spreadsheet popped up on the screen. "In fact, he's in the penthouse with Mariah as we speak."

"What's he doing there?" Kalum asked.

Hack pressed another key and a video display popped up beside the schedule showing a view looking into the penthouse suite from the balcony. "Looks like they're having breakfast."

"Breakfast?"

"I thought you said the penthouse had no cameras," Blemm said.

Hack grinned at him. "Bird's eye view."

Kalum came to Hack's side and looked at the screen. "She looks just the same as I remember. Why is Borlan having breakfast with her?"

Hack shrugged and squinted at the computer screen. "His schedule shows he meets her for breakfast every morning. After lunch today, which will be in the main dining hall, he's scheduled to approve some kind of goblin upgrades." He tapped the screen. "That interests me. I wonder what changes they've made. I can only hope they've made them smell better."

Hack sat back in his seat and crossed his arms. "So, I'm thinking the best time to attempt a rescue is at noon, the day after tomorrow when the tournament is just getting started. That's when the most people will be here, and all eyes, and cameras, will be focused on the gaming floor."

"Makes sense. Let's say midday, in two days' time."

Hack nodded. "But we have a lot of work to do before then. I've analyzed the tower's security, and there are a lot of doors that are controlled by handprint scanners. I can hotwire them as we encounter them, but it will take time."

"And you'll need to be here at the computer as our eyes sometimes," Kalum said. "Can you show us how to bypass the scanners?"

Hack nodded. "I can. But it would be easier if we could replicate a handprint that will access them."

"We could just cut the hand off a goblin," Blemm said.

Hack shook his head. "It's always a fight with you. Anyway, the scanners are set up for only certain goblins at certain times. A goblin hand won't work on all the scanners. I suspect Borlan's hand is the only one that will work every time."

Blemm grinned. "So we're going to cut off Borlan's hand?"

Hack shook his head. "I don't need his actual hand. I just need his handprint to make a duplicate."

Kalum scoffed. "How in Lorr are we supposed to get Borlan's handprint?"

"I have an idea on that," Trinn replied. "Hack, can you pull up a picture of the uniforms worn by the dining staff?"

Hack gave her a knowing smile and turned back to the computer.

Blemm cleared his throat. "Um. Off the subject, I have a rather important question," he said. "We're a long way up in this unseemly labyrinth. What happens, I mean, what are we supposed to do when… nature calls?"

They all grinned. Kalum stood. "Blemm, my old friend, come with me. I want to introduce you to something called *indoor plumbing*. You're gonna love it."

FIFTEEN

A DISTURBING DISCOVERY

THE MAIN DINING hall was empty of tower guests. No one was allowed inside while the king ate his afternoon meal. Borlan sat, bored and restless, sipping a glass of water and nibbling at the remains of his meal. Freedling sat across the table, reading endlessly from a datapad, updating the king on everything from the Tower's current inventory of sliced bread, to the status of the ironing being done on tablecloths.

"Freedling, please," Borlan groaned. "Isn't there anything interesting on that thing that you could share with me?"

Freedling looked up, confusion on his face. He looked back at the pad, back up at Borlan, and then back at the pad once again. "Interesting?" the man sniffed. Just then, the pad chimed as a message appeared on the screen. "Oh!" Freedling chirped. "Here's something. Elbore is here to see you, Your Majesty."

Borlan's eyes lit up. "Elbore?"

"Yes, Your Majesty."

"He's here?"

"Yes, Your Majesty."

"But I thought he was taking some time for himself down in Yawlingshire."

Freedling rolled his eyes. "He was, Your Majesty. And now... he's here. Shall I send him in?"

"Yes. Of course. Send him in at once."

Freedling tapped the screen of his pad and rose from his seat. "I'll be just outside, Your Majesty."

Borlan waved a dismissive hand at him. "Fine."

The king waited, eagerly watching the door. It had been weeks since he'd seen Elbore, and he looked forward to seeing some more of his magic. Magic was in rare supply these days since he'd banned its use entirely. Only the Dragons and Elbore himself were allowed to wield its power under the law. The Dragons were powerful but still not as amusing as Elbore.

"I'm sorry, Your Majesty," a red-haired servant woman had come beside him. "Your glass is smudged. Let me replace it." She picked up his water glass with a cloth napkin and replaced it with a new one. Borlan hadn't noticed any smudges on the glass, but he used the opportunity to exercise his authority.

"I should hope you're sorry," he snapped. "I won't tolerate this kind of ineptitude in the future. Do you understand me?"

The woman didn't respond, she was staring off into the distance. Borlan followed her gaze and saw that Elbore had come in and was shuffling his way to the table.

"Get out," he told the woman. "Get away!"

"Yes, Your Majesty." The woman hurried away as Elbore reached the table.

Borlan stood. "Elbore, my old friend. Please sit."

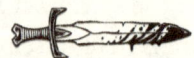

From a distant corner of the dining hall, Trinn stood, cloaked in illusion, quietly chanting the spell for enhanced hearing. She discretely let the water pour onto the floor from the glass she was holding before slipping it into a pocket. Finally, the voices of Borlan and the man he was meeting with became clear and loud in her ears.

"How were your travels?" Borlan asked.

"Not worth mentioning. I drank a lot."

"Elbore," Borlan sounded disappointed. "I thought you were going to use your time to sober yourself."

"Never mind my drinking," Elbore snapped. "I have news. I met a group of people who could create trouble for you."

A short while later, back in the room, Hack and the others listened as Trinn explained what she'd overheard. "It was Eli," she said.

"Wait. Eli is Elbore?" Hack said. "*The* Elbore?"

Trinn nodded. "Yes, and he told Borlan all about our plans to rescue Mariah. How does he even know? Did one of you tell him?"

They all shook their heads.

"He must have overheard us talking at the tavern," Kalum said, his hands on his head. "This changes everything. If Borlan knows we're here, we can't attempt a rescue."

"Now, hold on a second," Hack held up a finger. "Let's think about this. What does Borlan really know?"

"He knows we're coming, which gives him an advantage," Blemm said.

"He knows that *somebody* is going to attempt a rescue," Hack said, speaking slowly. "But he doesn't know who, and he doesn't know when or how. Only Eli, er Elbore, has seen our faces. And, with the exception of Trinn, who the entire kingdom is looking for, nobody knows where we are and is unlikely to find us. Trinn, did Eli say anything about our plans in detail?"

Trinn shook her head, "No. In fact, he told Borlan that he didn't have any details. He knows our names, though."

"That's okay," Hack said. "I'm the only one who actually checked in, and I didn't use my real name, although they'll probably put Hack and Mister Hax together. But that doesn't matter, because Mister Hax is currently staying three floors above us."

Kalum rubbed his chin. "Hmm. I suppose it's not as bad as it sounds, but if we're going to continue this, everyone needs to be extra careful. Do you understand?"

They all nodded.

"Well," Hack said. "Some good news is that Trinn managed to recover some very good prints from Borlan on this glass. I should be able to replicate his handprint pretty easily."

Kalum nodded, rubbing his eyes. "I need some sleep. We should all get some rest."

Hack shook his head. "I'm not tired."

Blemm went to one bed while Trinn took the other. Kalum lay back on the sofa and was asleep within seconds.

A few hours later, just a block away from the tower, King Borlan, with Freedling by his side, entered the Lorr Biomech Control Center. The LBCC was really just a squat, nondescript, concrete bunker with a five-story antenna mounted on its roof. Puxley was inside awaiting their arrival. He rose when he saw Borlan enter and unconsciously wiped away crumbs from his rumpled shirt and pushed his glasses up on his nose. Puxley was a Rhast. He'd relocated to Lorr shortly after the Day of Arrival, seeking a new life of adventure for him and his family. But he quickly fell into a life very much like the one he'd had in Rhastor, sitting in front of a computer screen all day long. Running system analysis of Lorr's biomech population day in and day out was far from the adventure he'd longed for, but he was good at his job, and every once in a while, he was given more interesting assignments such as the one they would be testing today.

"King Borlan, sir," Puxley stammered. "Thank you for coming. I think you're going to like what you see."

Borlan nodded. "As long as you've done what I asked."

"Oh, yes, sir. It's even better than I expected." Puxley rushed to a curtain on the wall behind him and pulled it aside revealing a large window. Beyond the window, Borlan could see a square concrete room. It was completely empty, save for one goblin biomech standing in the center.

"That's Test Subject 002, sir. It's been loaded with the new software and will demonstrate its new capabilities."

"Yes, yes. Let's get on with it," Borlan whined impatiently.

Puxley sat down at his computer and typed in an initiate command for the goblin. "The window here is two-inch thick reinforced polyglass. Very strong stuff."

Borlan nodded, clenching his fists. He hated to be kept waiting. Inside the room the biomech turned to face the window. Borlan saw its eyes flicker from yellow to green. Borlan's own eyes widened as he stared in anticipation of what was coming.

Puxley gave a short countdown. "Three. Two. One."

The sequence initiated in glorious fashion. Borlan's eyes bulged. "Gods," he gasped.

Puxley wore a proud smile.

The king's mouth moved up and down silently before he found his voice again. "How soon can you upload this to the rest?" he asked.

"Immediately."

Borlan nodded and turned to Freedling. "Give Puxley the names and information we have of our uninvited guests. I want any information he can find and any security footage we have of these people."

"Yes, Your Majesty," Freedling said as Borlan stormed out.

SIXTEEN

FORTUNATE FINDS

WHILE THE OTHERS napped, Hack used the opportunity to do a bit of shopping. He linked his datapad to the suite's computer and took it with him. Once he'd exited the building, he logged in and deleted all footage of himself leaving the tower.

Hack was in buyer's heaven. In a city like this, there was literally nothing that wasn't for sale. He bought himself a sweet drink and explored the perimeter streets around the tower. For all the reputed enchantment of Central City, the neighborhoods surrounding Lorr Tower were anything but glamorous. It was midday; still hours until electric lights and the dark of night would mask the garbage and unseemly scars that the daylight so cruelly exposed.

Hack had specific items he wanted to find, so he wasn't always successful on his first attempts. But he hit the jackpot on locating the most important item he needed. At an industrial supply shop called The Fool's Tools, Hack spent a small fortune on a tool he'd researched called a thermic bore. Along with the bore, he purchased a tripod for the device and a pair of protective goggles.

Next, he picked up some clothing items from a hole-in-the-wall thrift store. He knew the group would need disguises, so he bought clothes in all sizes: small for himself and Trinn; regular for Kalum; and humongous to accommodate Blemm's towering frame.

Returning to the streets, he looked for businesses of a seedier nature, where one could find goods not typically sought by respectable shoppers. It was in the Treasure Chest where he found a small wireless camera that would link perfectly to his datapad. It would come in handy to watch the fourteenth floor hallway outside the suite. At the King Takes Pawn Shop he found a universal network cable that he'd soon need, and in an unexpected surprise, he came across a device coyly labeled a Wave Crasher, which Hack knew was actually a gamma disruption grenade; harmless to people but a real headache for biomechs. The greasy-looking owner tallied his purchases.

"Got any more of these?" Hack asked, holding up the Wave Crasher.

The owner nodded. "Got a few more in the back."

"I'll take 'em."

"All right. Anything else?"

Hack shook his head. "Not unless you carry time locks for vault doors."

The owner's eyes brightened. "As a matter of fact, I've got a broken one if you're crafty enough to repair it. I'll sell it cheap. Otherwise I can order a new one. It'll take a week."

"That's very fortunate," Hack said. "I'll taken the broken one. I'm pretty crafty."

As the man rummaged beneath the counter for the lock, Hack's eyes fell upon a glass display case. Inside the case was the most mundane item one might see: a simple blue sack. The marking on the bag was shaped in an oddly circular design. Hack's eyes widened in recognition.

He pointed at the case. "Is that what I think it is?"

The man looked up and nodded. "Yep. My pride and joy. Only one of its kind in all of Northern Lorr."

"How'd you get it?"

"Wasn't easy," he replied.

"How much?"

The man laughed. "I promise you. It's worth more than you got."

Hack smiled at the man. "Try me."

When he arrived back at the tower, all of his items carried nicely in his new blue bag, Hack went straight to the elevator, intent on returning to the room. But once inside the lift, his curiosity was piqued by the button labeled B: *Tower Personnel Only.* The vault was in the basement, he knew. Kalum had warned him that the mission was to save Mariah, not rob the vault, but Hack had decided early on that the opportunity was too good not to take a crack at it. Kalum couldn't be mad at him when they finished their mission with a ton more gold than they had expected. He pressed the button for the basement. He wanted to see if he could get a look at the vault up close.

The bell chimed as the door slid open. Hack readied himself. He had no idea what kind of security was down here. If he was caught, he'd simply claim he'd gotten lost. Sometimes, the simplest plans were best.

But instead of a hoard of goblins, a man dressed in coveralls and carrying a small toolbox stood waiting for the lift to arrive. The badge on his chest indicated he was with the Maintenance Group. Hack nodded nonchalantly to him and exited the elevator.

"Wait a second," the man said as he passed, grabbing Hack by the shoulder. "This floor is for Tower employees only."

Hack looked at the man. "That's right." He moved in a flash, sweeping the man's arm behind him with his own arm and pushing him against the wall. He hit him hard at the base of his neck, snapping his head back and rendering him unconscious.

Hack dragged the man into the open lift. Keying the button to close the door, he immediately got to work relieving the man of his maintenance uniform.

Minutes later, wearing coveralls several sizes too large for him, Hack made his way through the basement corridors. He navigated the halls from memory of the plans he'd studied. He passed by the arid heat of the laundry area and smelled the aroma of fresh baking as he passed the kitchen. Strange, he thought, that the corridors were so empty.

Even stranger was when he reached his destination to find the vault door standing wide open. The room had an open entrance, and there were no cameras and no guards of any kind by the vault. Something was wrong. It had been far too easy to get to where he was standing. Either the Tower had much poorer security than he'd imagined or something was going on.

Stepping with caution in case there was someone inside, Hack made his way to the open vault. His heart sank as he stepped inside to find the shelves stacked not with gold but with food. His mind spun with questions. What was going on? Who locks up food in a vault? Where was the gold?

As he made his way back to the elevator, he was met by a kitchen worker coming off her shift. "Excuse me," Hack said. "I was told to check out the vault, but it appears it's being used for other purposes."

The woman nodded. "Been a kitchen storage locker for about a year now. Ever since the remodel. But we don't ever use it much."

Hack laughed. "Well, I'm definitely in the wrong place, then. Do you happen to know where the new vault is located?"

The woman shook her head. "Nobody does. 'Cept the goblins, and we don't talk to them much." Her eyes darted to the badge on the uniform. "Hey, shouldn't a maintenance guy know where the vault is?"

Hack nodded. "Absolutely, he should." Then with a wink, he said, "Don't tell anyone, okay? Our little secret."

The woman smiled at him as he turned and continued on to the elevator. He'd gone just a few feet when he noticed a goblin coming up the corridor toward him. Damn. With a deep breath, he steeled his confidence and walked straight at the goblin. As he moved left to pass the biomech, it stopped. *<No maintenance is scheduled in this area,>* the goblin said. *<Are you authorized to be here?>*

Hack smiled and put on a heavy drawl. "Just stopped by the kitchen to say hello to my old lady. Got myself all turned around. Where is that confounded elevator?"

The goblin stared at him for several seconds, and Hack was beginning to think he'd been caught. But then it turned and pointed. *<It's that way.>*

Hack nodded. "Thank you, officer."

When Hack returned to the suite, the others were still sleeping. He parked himself again at the computer and continued his research into the Tower's security.

Kalum, who'd been sleeping on the couch, awoke a half hour later with a yawn.

"Oh, sorry, Kalum," Hack said. "I hope I didn't wake you."

Kalum sat up and rubbed his eyes. "No. Don't you ever get tired?"

"Not really," Hack replied with a grin and pointed to the pile of items on the table. "I went shopping."

Kalum glanced over the pile. Several boxes sat upon a stack of clothing. Kalum got up and examined the purchases. "What are these?" Kalem asked, holding up one of the Wave Crashers.

Hack looked up from his screen. "Oh. Those are gamma disruption grenades. Thought they might come in handy."

"Grenades?" Kalum shouted, dropping the box back on the table as if it might bite him. "Why would you buy these things?"

"Don't worry," Hack said, surprised by his reaction. "They aren't explosive. They can't hurt you, unless you're a goblin."

"We don't need them," Kalum said flatly. "We've never used grenades before. Get rid of them."

Kalum closed his eyes and took a long breath. "I'm sorry, Hack. I shouldn't have snapped at you. I suppose this mission has me on edge."

Hack waved a hand at him, dismissively. "Oh, who cares. Come take a look at this."

Kalum rubbed the last of the sleep from his eyes. He felt bad for the way he'd spoken to Hack and worse that he couldn't explain his feelings. He followed Hack to the computer.

Just then, Blemm came out of the bedroom looking unrested. "What's all the clamor?" he grumbled.

Hack was in his chair rubbing his hands together. "Come check this out," he said. "Remember, I told you about the priority system they use for the cameras? Well look at this."

He brought up a number of windows on the screen. "This list is of the current priority cameras." He pointed to the list. "In other words, these are the cameras that are currently being actively watched by security."

Kalum nodded.

"Okay." Hack pointed at a video showing a card table in the gambling hall. "This camera here is sixth in priority. This video is actually from a few minutes ago. See this guy here in the gray tunic?"

Kalum looked and saw the gray-shirted man Hack was referring to. His back was to the camera as he sat at one of the poker tables playing a hand. "Yeah, I see him."

"Well, what you can't see from the camera's angle is that he's got a datalink on his lap that he's using to cheat."

"Lot of good that camera's doing," Blemm said, looking on.

"Exactly," said Hack. "But see this goblin over here?" He pointed at a goblin in the video. "It does see him cheating." He pointed back to the priority list. "Now, watch this?"

It happened fast, but Kalum saw it. The top camera in the priority list changed to *GOB087* and bumped all the other cameras down one spot. The camera they'd been watching moved down to seventh priority. Within seconds the video feed showed a team of goblins swarming on the man and ushering him away.

"Did you see it?"

"Yeah." Kalum nodded. "The goblin took highest priority

on the list. But, what does that mean?"

"It means," Hack swiveled in his chair to face them, "that the goblins are linked to the security system. It means that any goblin can decide to override the priority algorithm whenever it wants. It makes sense. If a goblin sees something happening, he can get that info to security in an instant."

"So, how is this great?" Kalum asked. "Sounds to me like one more problem to deal with. No, wait—two hundred more problems."

"No," Hack said. "You're missing the point. If we can get enough goblins to take notice of something, something big, they'll override the entire priority list. Meaning—"

"Meaning," Kalum said, suddenly understanding. "They won't be watching the important cameras. Like the ones where we'll be."

"Exactly!"

Kalum turned to Blemm. "Have you figured out that distraction we talked about?"

Blemm scratched at his moustache. "I think so. It should do the trick."

"Can you time it for the start of the tournament?"

Blemm nodded. "Sure, but there's something else I'd like to take care of before then. Can I borrow your car?"

Kalum blinked. "Blemm, have you ever driven a car before?"

Blemm looked deeply offended. "Of course I've driven before! What, you think a potato farmer can't drive a car?"

Kalum apologized for his misassumption, feeling more guilty that he'd managed to offend both of his friends within minutes. He handed Blemm the key. "Don't park it in any bad neighborhoods, okay?"

SEVENTEEN

THE GOBLIN, GLORTT

IT WAS TECHNICALLY not a lie that Blemm had driven a car. He'd driven his neighbor's new truck years before on his farm. Unfortunately, he had driven it exactly thirty-one feet, in a straight line, directly into a tree. So it was a challenge at best to navigate Kalum's car out of the parking lot without doing damage to it or to others.

Now, on the open road, Blemm felt more at ease. He'd grown accustomed to using the accelerator and cruised along at a steady pace, feeling greater confidence in his driving prowess with each passing mile. He even received a compliment on his driving from a fellow driver, who had followed closely on his tail for some time, finally racing up alongside and yelling out to him, "Nice driving, Grandpa!"

Blemm waved at the man and replied, "Thank you," before adding, "but, I have no grandchildren."

It wasn't long before he reached the area he sought. He'd noticed the oddly stacked rocks beside the road as they were coming out of the Atlas Mountains that morning. He'd recognized it as a goblin place marker and noted its location. He pulled the car off the road and set out on foot, following a barely noticeable pathway that led along the base of a sharp cliff.

It wasn't long before the path ended at a solid rock face in the mountain. Scanning the carved surface with his eyes and running his fingers over each groove and indention, he at last located a crude triangular design carved to look like a natural fissure in the rock. This was the goblin symbol for *"entrance,"* or more accurately, *"opening to go through."* He looked back to make sure he was hidden from the road and then pressed a finger into the center of the triangle and grunted, "Gluk Splurt," which in Goblish, meant, *"Reveal this hidden door and let me in."*

Blemm stepped back as the rock face split, a jagged crack ripping down from the top to the ground. With a grinding rumble, the crack widened. It shifted and crumbled, revealing a slim opening. The opening was narrow, but with a bit of contortion, he managed to squeeze inside.

The cavern was dark and small, built for goblin sizes, and Blemm crouched low, practically crawling to avoid scraping his head on the ceiling. The walls were embedded with a scattering of tiny green gems that glowed in the darkness, and his eyes were slow to adjust. He crawled through narrow tunnels, guided only by the glowing rocks, like a portal of stars, until finally the cramped passage opened into an enormous cavern. The high ceiling drooped with stalactites, and water dripped all around, each droplet echoing in tones on the rocky floor, creating a strange rhythmic orchestra of sound.

"Stay where you are!" a voice spat in Goblish. Blemm spun around to find three goblins, each with a spear pointed in his direction.

"How he get in?" one of them asked in a short series of burps.

Blemm spoke in heavily accented Goblish. *"I carry no weapon."*

The goblins stiffened in surprise. *"You speak the tongue!"* one grunted. In the dim glow, their green skin looked gray like wet stone, but their yellow eyes shone brightly.

"I was a friend to Glach, son of Glortt. I am here to pay my respects."

They lowered their spears but kept their distance. *"First you pay gold, then pay respects."*

Blemm retrieved a few gold coins from a pouch at his waist and tossed them on the ground. *"Now, take me to Glortt!"* he demanded and spit on the ground. He knew his gruff demand would be taken as a show of esteem for the goblin ways and not with any disrespect.

The goblin in front turned to one of the others. *"Tell Glortt. We bring."* The goblin turned and scurried off into shadows.

"Follow," the first goblin told Blemm. *"Follow slow."*

They led him along a series of rocky bridges that crossed the watery sludge that covered the cavern floor. They stopped on a flat platform in the center of the cave.

"Who are you?" came a thunderous voice. Blemm looked up to see a hunched and haggard goblin. He was grossly fat and his face was heavily scarred.

"I am Blemm, friend of Glach."

"Blemm," the fat goblin repeated his name. *"I remember Glach tell. Good you were to Glach."*

Blemm nodded. *"Glach was good. I come to offer my sorrow."*

"I am Glortt, King of Seekers. Thank you. Glach died well killing machines."

Blemm nodded. *"We must all fight machines. Time now to stop hiding."*

They spoke for a long time. They spoke of the old days and they spoke of the future. Blemm gained a better understanding and greater respect for the goblins. He left Glortt with a promise of hope, an offer of help, and a chance for the Seekers to regain some of their lost glory.

Borlan sat at a computer screen in his make-shift office, the one he was using while Mariah remained a prisoner in the penthouse. The screen was filled with the unseemly face of Puxley.

"What is it, Puxley?" Borlan groaned.

"Your Majesty," Puxley replied. "I've gone through the video archives and can't seem to find any footage of the group you're seeking."

Borlan frowned. "So, you're saying they never came into the tower?"

Puxley shook his head. "No, sir, I'm not saying that. Not necessarily. It appears that several minutes of video has been deleted from the archive. Starting around the timeframe that Mister Freedling said they would have arrived."

"Deleted?"

"Yes, sir. Lobby footage is missing from all cameras at that time. And then elevator footage appears to have been deleted for the period shortly after."

Borlan's eyes narrowed in anger. "You're telling me we have nothing?"

"Well," Puxley stammered. "I did find something interesting when I cross-referenced the check-ins for that morning. A Mister Hax checked in to a suite on the seventeenth floor earlier that morning. I only noticed it because the name is so similar to one of the names Freedling gave me—"

"Hack." Borlan smiled.

"Yes, sir."

"Thank you, Puxley." Borlan's smile widened. "That's very helpful."

EIGHTEEN

SECURITY SERVERS
AT SUNSET

WHILE BLEMM WAS conversing with goblins, the others took the opportunity to carry out the first step in their plans. In the parking lot of the Tower, Hack stood leaning against the side of a truck. He watched the shadows growing longer on the tall building as the sun set lower in the sky. Everything had to be timed perfectly for this to work. Kalum was waiting in the driver's seat, and hopefully, Trinn had gained access to the fourth floor rooftop landing of the tower that faced the adjacent Server Building. He checked the time on his wrist before returning his attention to the growing shadows. The tower was now draped in a checkerboard of sunlight and shadows.

Hack's mind wandered, admiring the grand design of the tower. The ground floor was skirted by large awnings of sparkling gold. On every odd numbered floor above that, each room was adorned with a large rectangular balcony, so in late afternoon the shadows created from these railed outcroppings checkered the building to fabulous effect. Hack gazed as the shadows stretched into perfect squares, completing the design: a perfect checkerboard.

Hack pressed a button on his datalink and spoke. "All right. Time to go." He jumped up on the side of the truck and held on, gripping the top. The truck was a large maintenance vehicle he'd just rented nearby. It was large enough to briefly block the security cameras mounted on the tower that watched the entrance to the Server Building.

He heard Kalum's voice respond from his wrist. "Okay. Trinn, we're on our way." The trucked rolled slowly along the alleyway between the tower and the Server Building. They'd waited for the sun to reach the perfect angle to produce the proper glare on the cameras. Hack's hope was that the glare would obscure the view enough for Trinn's illusion to go unnoticed.

As they approached the Server Building, Hack saw the front of the building waver momentarily, and Kalum slowed the truck to a crawl as they came between the cameras and the entrance. Hack jumped from the side of the truck and dashed headlong into the building's wall. For an instant, he worried that he was about to collide with solid brick, but then he was through. He stopped and looked about. He appeared to be standing in a narrow slot between two identical buildings—one, the actual Server Building, and the other, a backside of the illusion Trinn had created, which was an exact duplicate of the building standing three feet back so that the cameras would see the mock building instead of Hack entering the real one. It was odd seeing the backside of an illusion, something he'd never experienced before.

Affixing the fake gel palm print he'd created to his own right hand, Hack palmed the scanner beside the doors. He heard the satisfying click as the electronic locks disengaged. He rushed inside, wasting not a second, as Trinn had told him maintaining such a large illusion would be tiring, and she didn't know how long she could keep it up.

He keyed his datalink again. "I'm inside," he told the others. Looking ahead into the long aisle of racks and panels alive with blinking lights, he saw the web of red beams crisscrossing the way. He moved quickly to a security panel mounted just inside the doors and again placed his fabricated palm against a scanner.

The panel door popped open and Hack easily disengaged the sensor beams and motion detectors that guarded the equipment.

It took him a few minutes to identify which server racks controlled the tower operations, the ones he already had access to, and which ones controlled the secure equipment, like camera operation and elevator control. Using the link cable he'd purchased earlier, he connected the two racks, bridging communication between them. He quickly tucked the excess length of cable between racks, hiding it as best he could. Having double-checked his work, he rushed back out of the building, stopping only to reactivate the security measures.

"I'm ready to go," he informed the others, and then he waited behind Trinn's illusionary façade until he heard Kalum say, "Now!"

Charging through the illusion, he jumped back onto the side of the truck that Kalum had turned around and driven back up the alley. Everything had gone perfectly. "All clear, Trinn," he signaled. "Great job."

Trinn breathed a sigh of relief as she let down the illusion she'd been holding for too long. A wave of exhaustion fell over her. She didn't blame Hack for taking as long as he did, he'd surely moved as quickly as he could, but the energy required for such magic had taken its toll and she was spent. She made her way back to the doorway that led back inside, looking forward to a restful night's sleep.

As she entered the door, she had a fraction of a second to see Skinner and another man, a large man, blocking her way, before the bigger one punched her hard in the face. The last thing she remembered was wondering how long it would take for her broken nose to heal.

Four biomech goblins stood quietly outside the door to the suite. They had approached with caution, moving slowly to soften their heavy footsteps. Now in position, the lead goblin nodded to one of the others. With a thunderous kick, the biomech burst open the door and the entire team stormed inside. The suite was dark, and the goblins stumbled into furniture until one keyed the button for lights. The suite was empty. Aside from the bumped and displaced furniture caused by the goblins' entry, the room appeared to be untouched. The lead goblin transmitted a message to Tower Security: *Suite 1724 unoccupied. Schedule Maintenance for door repair.*

NINETEEN

BORLAN'S BACKSTABBING

ELBORE WALKED AT Borlan's side as they made their way through the crowded lobby of the tower. It was late, but gamblers from all over were already arriving for the tournament. Each wore that burning gleam of hope in their eyes; the one that would surely be stomped out before they left again.

"I've done a bit of research, Your Majesty, and I've discovered something I think you'll find interesting," Elbore said.

"I'm listening," Borlan replied.

"Kalum Tinbrook, Your Majesty. He's the one leading the group of rescuers."

"The name seems familiar," Borlan said. "What about him?"

"It appears he was once in a serious relationship with Mariah, Baron Rothburn's daughter."

Borlan stopped. "Yes, I remember now." His eyes wandered about aimlessly. "I'm beginning to suspect it was the baron himself who sent these so-called rescuers in the first place."

Elbore rolled his eyes. *Of course it was the baron!* "Your deductive reasoning is astonishing, sir."

Borlan smiled, oblivious to the sarcasm. "I think it's time to turn up Rothburn's sense of urgency. Have Puxley send a message to the baron telling him that his pitiful attempt at rescue has failed. Tell him Kalum Tinbrook and his friends are dead."

"Shouldn't we wait until we actually capture them, sir?" Elbore said.

"It doesn't matter. We'll have them soon enough. Tell him

that because of his meddling, I'm moving up the date of Mariah's execution. That ought to raise the pressure enough for him to be reasonable."

"What if he tries to contact this Kalum Tinbrook directly?"

Borlan nodded. "You're right, Elbore. Tell Puxley I want all electronic communications in and out of the tower blocked."

"Sir," Elbore said. "There are over a thousand guests that will be affected by that."

Borlan shrugged. "Who cares? Anyway, it will only be for a few days, for I suspect we'll get a response from Rothburn very quickly."

"Yes, sir."

"Thank you, Elbore," Borlan said, moving again toward the elevators. "It's good to have you back."

"Your Majesty is too kind," Elbore bowed his head slightly. "On the subject of my return, I have a request. These past years, have I not done everything you've asked of me? Have I not been a loyal servant?"

Borlan nodded. "You've been a fine companion. And a great magician."

They reached the elevator and Borlan keyed the button to call the lift.

"Then, I ask you to keep your end of our deal and return my wife and daughter."

Borlan looked at Elbore with an unreadable expression, but he quickly looked away. "Well, that will take some time, Elbore. I'll need to send a communication to the Rhast, and their journey back to Lorr will take days at least."

The elevator door opened and they entered the lift.

"I've waited years already. What's a few more days?"

Borlan palmed the scanner in the lift and the doors closed. His eyes darted nervously this way and that, and Elbore suspected that the king was being deceitful.

"That is," Elbore said, watching Borlan's eyes carefully, "if they're indeed still alive."

Borlan's eyes widened and flashed to Elbore's, then just as quickly to the floor. And Elbore knew that the king's next words would be a lie.

"Of course they're alive," Borlan said with a nervous laugh.

Elbore felt his knees about to buckle. They were already dead; or at least Borlan believed they were. The bell chimed inside the lift and the door slid open. A trio of goblins stood guard just outside the elevator.

"I'll send a communication to the Rhast at once," Borlan said as he exited the lift. Elbore stepped out as well and watched the king walk away down the narrow corridor looking absently at the datalink on his wrist. A blackness crept over Elbore's heart and he felt his power rising. Nothing would be easier than to strike him down right here in his own fortress. But it was not the time and it was not the place.

Suddenly Borlan turned. He looked back at Elbore watching him. For a moment, his brow furrowed. Did he suspect what Elbore was thinking?

The king's chin lifted. "Elbore," he called. He lifted his arm, indicating his datalink. "Come with me. I told you we'd get them. We have the woman."

Hack worked furiously at the computer, trying not to be distracted by Kalum's pacing. Trinn had been captured. They'd waited an hour, sending her message after message, but they had received no reply. Voice communication was restricted within the tower, so they had to rely upon text, but wherever she was, she was either unwilling or unable to respond.

Poring through the tower's camera footage, Hack had located video of Trinn being accosted by Skinner and another man.

"How does Skinner keep finding her?" Kalum asked. "First at the tavern and now here?"

Hack shook his head. "He must be tracking her somehow."

The video showed they'd taken her to a room on the ninth floor and waited until Borlan arrived with Elbore. From there, Trinn was carried to a lift where they all got inside and that's where they lost her.

The elevator footage showed the five of them go into the elevator, and then Borlan, instead of pressing one of the floor buttons, placed his palm against a flat surface of the panel. The camera immediately turned off after that.

"It's obviously a palm scanner," Hack said, reviewing the footage again, "but made to not look like one."

Blemm returned to the suite then, and they filled him in on what had happened.

"And you have no idea where they took her?" Blemm asked.

Hack shook his head. "There's no camera. No floor indicator. I can't even locate any footage of them getting off the elevator. I've looked at every floor for the five minutes after they got in. Nothing." Hack banged a hand on the desktop. "I've gone back through the archives and I found the same thing every time. Borlan gets into an elevator. And then he just vanishes. There must be a secret floor."

"Well, we have the fake handprint," Kalum said. "I'll just go see where it takes me."

Hack stood and went to the window. "I don't like it," he said. "I hate you walking into a completely blind situation. What if there's another dragon?"

"We don't really have a choice, Hack. Trinn's in trouble and we have to get her."

Blemm nodded in agreement. "We can't leave her to face whatever villainy Borlan has in store."

Hack nodded. "Okay, but you're going to wear the camera. There are obviously no cameras where you're going, and I want to know what's happening in case you end up needing rescuing as well. I've made a duplicate of the handprint, so if you get in a bind, Blemm and I can come after you. And you're taking a disruption grenade, no arguments."

Kalum looked like he was going to object, but then he nodded. "Fine."

"Good," Hack said. "I've linked the camera directly to my datapad, so as long as this secret floor isn't a hundred feet underground, the connection should be clear."

"All right," Kalum said, affixing the small camera to his tunic and clipping the grenade to his belt. "Okay. I'm ready."

"Wait," Hack said. "You might need this." He held up a black glove. "See? I attached Borlan's palm print right to the glove. Makes it easier than having to glue it to your hand each time."

Kalum took the glove. "Thanks, Hack. Wish me luck."

After Kalum left, Hack turned back to the window. Luck. He didn't believe in luck. It was just a superstitious notion, like Blemm's fear of being on the thirteenth floor.

He blinked. Thirteenth floor. He stepped closer to the window and looked down to the balcony of the suite below them and to the bottom of the balcony above. "Our room has no balcony," he muttered. His mind raced. *Secret floor... Checkerboard shadows....*

"Blemm," Hack turned. "Good news and bad news."

"Let's hear it," Blemm mumbled, clearly taking little interest in Hack's games.

"You needn't worry about bad luck. We aren't on the thirteenth floor after all."

Blemm nodded. "That *is* good news. We don't need that kind of bad luck. So, what's the bad news?"

"I think Kalum's on his way to the thirteenth floor now."

Puxley stood in the Biomech Command Center and looked admiringly on the various devices that lined the nondescript metal shelf in the corner. Over the years, in his spare time, he'd made a hobby of tinkering with some of the spare equipment that was inevitably left lying around. He was a Rhast, of course, and building things was in his blood, he supposed. He imagined one day inventing something that would make a real difference.

The tone chimed on his computer, indicating that a new message had arrived. He sat and keyed the incoming communication. His eyes widened. It was from the Rhast High Command. He read and reread the message before sitting back in his chair, exasperated. *What in the world is happening?* The message was an order to initiate a new command to the biomechs. He'd received commands for the goblins before but never directly from High Command, and this was unlike anything he'd seen before. *Well, the High Command must have their reasons.* He took a deep breath and deleted the message before getting started on this new assignment.

TWENTY

TRINN'S TENACITY

PAIN.

Trinn opened her eyes to excruciating light. An electric bulb shone brightly in front of her. Her head throbbed in aching misery. She was seated in a chair, her arms resting on a table in front of her.

"Ah, there she is," a man's voice cooed gently. She felt the touch of a warm damp cloth against her lips. "Take it easy," said the voice. "You're fine for now. Just a bit of blood."

She struggled to remember. Where was she? How did she get here? She squinted into the light, but she couldn't make out the face of the man sitting across from her. She started to ask where she was but found she couldn't speak. Something was in her mouth, cold and firm. It seemed to be strapped around her head. A gag of some kind?

"Don't try to talk," said the voice. "It's no use."

She moved to stand, but she found she was bound to the chair as well. Her arms were tied down to the surface of the table. She struggled and pulled, but the chair and table were both firmly attached to the floor. She was completely restrained.

"Settle down now. You're being held for all of our protection. I need to ask you some questions and I don't want you interrupting me with your magic."

Magic. She remembered. An image of Skinner flashed in her mind. He was here, in the tower. How?

"It's funny really," said the man. "For years, we experimented with electrical gizmos to try and block a magic user's concentration so they couldn't cast spells. They never worked. Then one day, a good friend of mine informed me that for a spell to work, it must be spoken. It was so simple. If you can't speak, no magic. Hence the gag. I'm sorry if it's uncomfortable."

Trinn squinted, trying to see the man, but the glare from the bulb was too great. She already had a suspicion of who it was anyway.

"Here, dear, let me turn off this light. I can see it's bothering you."

The light clicked off and Trinn blinked repeatedly until her eyes adjusted. As she suspected, it was Borlan, a smug smile on his face, sitting across the small table. "Do you know who I am?"

Trinn nodded. As her eyes grew more focused, she realized another man stood behind Borlan; an older man. It was Eli. Elbore.

"Good." He leaned forward and spoke in a hushed voice. "Sometimes people don't recognize their own king. Isn't that something?"

Trinn tried to say she'd recognize an ugly troll like him anywhere, but her mouth couldn't form the words.

Borlan shook his head. "See there, even after I told you it was no use to try and speak, you go ahead and do it anyway. What is it with you magic users? You seem to have no respect for authority." He turned to look at Elbore. "Present company excluded, of course."

Elbore looked on but gave no indication that he'd been spoken to.

Borlan turned back to face Trinn. "As king, I passed a law that forbid the use of magic, under punishment of death by fire. Fire! And even that doesn't stop you."

He sat back in his chair, a hand to his chin. "I know. You don't understand what death by fire really means, do you? You can't comprehend what it would feel like to be set on fire. I mean, that's understandable, who could? But maybe…" He reach up and clicked a switch. Trinn snapped her eyes shut as the blinding bulb flared back to light.

"Maybe you just need a taste of what that would be like. Then maybe you'd understand the consequences and would abandon your magic."

She opened one eye and saw Borlan had stood and was unhooking the lightbulb's cord from the hook that suspended it. He lowered the bulb until it rested on the top of Trinn's hand. The searing pain was shocking. She clamped her eyes shut but didn't struggle. It would do her no good, and she didn't want to give him the satisfaction.

After a second or two, Borlan lifted the bulb. "Goodness, that must hurt." He clicked off the light again and set it aside on the table. "Now, try to imagine that feeling over every inch of your body." He shook his head with a short laugh. "I'll tell you, that's a sensation I never want to endure."

The deep red mark on her hand still burned agonizingly, and Trinn blinked away the tears that flooded her eyes.

"I'm sorry." Borlan turned in his chair. "I've neglected to introduce you to my friend Elbore." He looked back at her. "But then, you've already met, haven't you?"

Trinn looked at the familiar man she knew as Eli. He stood motionless, expressionless, watching.

"It was Elbore who identified you as one of the criminals who destroyed my goblins in Midvale."

He leaned in over the table. "Now, Elbore is allowed to do magic. He's one of a small group that I have personally given my permission. You, on the other hand," he poked a finger at her injured nose, igniting another explosion of pain, "are not."

"Did you know," Borlan continued, "that Elbore can create fire with his magic? Fire that would make the burn of this lightbulb feel like a warm bath. But we'll come back to that."

He straightened his shoulders and faced her. "I want to know where your friends are hiding: Hack, Blemm, and Kalum Tinbrook. I know you came here with them, and you're going to tell me where to find them."

With a flick of his finger, Borlan switched on the burning hot bulb again.

Kalum entered the lift and pressed his gloved hand against the flat panel as he'd watched Borlan do in the video. The doors shut and the elevator began moving. Downward. Kalum wondered how far down he was headed. He was just remembering Hack's words, *as long as this secret floor isn't a hundred feet underground,* and starting to feel a bit claustrophobic when the lift stopped. Kalum looked. The indicator above the panel said 13.

The lift bell chimed as the door opened and Kalum readied his sword.

TWENTY ONE

GOBSLAYER

ELBORE STOOD IN the corner of the room and watched as Borlan tortured the woman. Again and again he pressed the white-hot bulb to her hand. The wound had blistered badly, and as he pulled the bulb away this last time, the scorched and blackened skin came away with it. Trinn, having admirably concealed her torment, now screamed out a terrible muffled cry through the gag. Elbore winced at the sight, thinking of his wife, so kind and so loving. He thought of his daughter, so beautiful and so innocent. Had they endured such torture? Borlan had taken them as insurance that Elbore would remain in his service, assuring him that his family would be returned in due time if Elbore remained loyal and obedient. Now, it seemed clear that Borlan had lied. His family was surely dead. But if there was even the slightest chance that they survived, and there was, he would find them.

There had been three goblins outside the lift as Kalum had exited. He had dispatched them quickly but not quickly enough. One managed to transmit its distress call. Now, Kalum fought his way through a seemingly endless onslaught of biomechs. He slashed and spun and ducked and stabbed his way along the corridor, leaving a growing trail of goblin wreckage as he went. With each kill-strike he felt the uncomfortable jolt through his body.

Goblins continued to appear in front of him, from doorways

and side corridors, their yellow eyes glowing bright in the dim passage. Their eyes blinked red as they signaled for more help, but every so often, a goblin's eyes flared green. Kalum had no idea what the green eyes indicated, but he wasn't eager to find out. GOBSlayer whirled mercilessly, cutting deeply to their steel goblin frames and scrambling thoroughly their goblin brains. Soon, sweat began to form on his face and the jolts from GOBSlayer's discharge became painful. He wiped the stinging sweat from his eyes.

As he spun to avoid a thrusted sword, his eyes caught glimpse of a trio of armored goblins down a side corridor. They turned to face him, their eyes immediately flashing red. He turned around, wishing he had eyes in back of his head as goblins came at him from every direction. More goblins' eyes were turning green as they approached him and Kalum began to wonder if they were filming, or broadcasting, or perhaps simply seeing in a different spectrum of light. Could the color change indicate a danger? He'd never encountered a green-eyed goblin before this day, and it bothered him to be doing battle against an unknown threat.

His breathing was coming hard and fast now. He whirled GOBSlayer again, this time slicing the transmitter nose from a red-eyed goblin before cutting into its neck. Its eyes went dark and it collapsed beside him as another jolt made Kalum wince. All the while, he searched, looking for a sign of where Trinn might be held. He'd passed several rooms already, but this wasn't the time to stop and knock on doors. A goblin sword slashed him across the shoulder and he spun to destroy it.

A disturbing thought came creeping into Kalum's mind as he checked the wound on his shoulder. What if Trinn was someplace else entirely? What if this was all for naught? It didn't matter now. This floor was the best chance he currently had of finding her, and even if he had to go through a thousand goblins to do it, he would find her.

TWENTY TWO

ELBORE'S ENTREATMENT

TRINN'S SUFFERING WAS beyond measure, but she still managed to hold on. She channeled the pain she felt into anger and hope. Anger at Borlan. And hope that help was coming. The others would find her somehow; that one thought she held strongly in her mind. They'd find her. Help was coming.

Borlan smacked her across the face. "Look at me," he shouted. "Tell me where your friends are?"

She stared at him, hatred in her eyes, and she was pleased to see he couldn't keep eye contact. He had her under a position of power, and still he was a coward, a weakling. But she nodded.

"Are they in the tower?" Borlan asked.

She shook her head, trying to just buy herself more time. Help was coming.

"I know somebody checked in under the name, Mr. Hax," Borlan said. "I know that was a friend of yours. But the room is empty. Did they go some place else?"

Trinn shook her head, intentionally sowing confusion. If she could get him to remove the gag, she might be able to use her magic before he could stop her.

"They're still in the building?" he shouted.

She shook her head again, watching his frustration rise.

A rumble of noise rose from outside the room.

"Damn it." He looked at Elbore, who was watching the situation, his hand over his mouth. "Find out what the hell is going…on…out…thh…" Borlan's head drooped forward as his eyes fell shut and he slumped in his chair, unconscious.

Elbore rushed forward and untied the gag from Trinn's mouth. "The sleep spell is strong, but do nothing that could wake him. We have to get you out of here. There are no fewer than fifty goblins on this floor."

Trinn gasped as the gag was removed. "Why are you…?"

"Why am I helping you?" Elbore looked surprised by the question. "Magic users have suffered greatly under King Borlan." His face scrunched up as his eyes welled with tears. "He took my family from me. He took them away to keep me loyal, and I did nothing to save them. Now I fear they're dead. I've been on the wrong side for too long." He wiped at his eyes and sniffed. "The kingdom needs people like you, Trinn. Show them. Show them the good that magic can do."

The noise outside grew louder, mechanical goblin voices muddled together.

"What will you do?" Trinn asked Elbore. "Won't he hurt you?"

"He can't hurt me any more than he has already. Anyway, I'm not staying either. I'm going to find my family. I'm going to Rhastor."

"Rhastor?"

Elbore nodded, working to untie Trinn from her binds.

"Thank you for—" She winced, the pain from the burn on her hand flaring angrily.

Elbore took her injured hand, spoke a short incantation, and the pain eased. "That will help for a while. Do you know any healing magic?"

She shook her head. "Not really."

"Then I'm sorry. You're in for a painful recovery." He held a hand near her face and cast another spell. "I don't think it's broken. Can you stand?"

Trinn nodded as she rose, her legs weak and shaky. She looked down at the sleeping king, and the anger she'd been gathering overflowed. She spoke words of magic and a glowing fireball flared between her outstretched hands. She lifted it above her head, preparing to hurl it down on the miserable king.

"Trinn Shadowmoon," Elbore said softly.

Trinn looked up. Elbore was staring at her, a peaceful expression on his face. "You're no killer."

She let the fireball vanish, her own words spoken to Skinner echoing in her ears: *I'm not a murderer.*

"Now, let's get you out of here," Elbore said, taking hold of the door handle. "I have a feeling all this commotion is for you."

Trinn took a deep breath and steeled her nerves. "Okay, I'm ready."

Kalum was just finishing off another green-eyed goblin when he saw her. Trinn stepped into the corridor some twenty feet ahead. She looked battered and weak, but there was fire in her eyes. In fact, there was fire in her hands as well. Fireballs, hot and wicked, she launched one after another at the goblins still surging toward Kalum. The corridor behind him was growing dense with goblins as more continued to flood into the passageway. Having fought his way all the way up the hall, it seemed he'd now have to fight his way back.

From the doorway through which Trinn had come, another came into the corridor. It was Eli, or Elbore, his arms outstretched inside of a glowing orb of blue light. As he stepped beside her, the light passed through her until she was also encompassed inside the orb. But when one goblin charged them, carrying a sparking stunstick, it literally bounced off the orb as if hitting a brick wall. The goblin lay stunned on the floor until Trinn ignited it in an explosion of flames.

Kalum felt the stinging heat of each fireball as Trinn sent them sizzling past him. He was panting for breath. The corridor began to darken further with the smoke and the stench of burning biomechs. Seeing an open path, he ran to Trinn and Elbore. Stopping before the blue light, he gingerly reached out to the orb, and somehow his hand was also able to pass through. He stepped inside.

"Are you all right?" he asked Trinn.

"Been better," she answered, launching another fireball. She looked at him. "Kalum, are you okay? You look awful."

"Keep moving," Elbore shouted as he started his way up the passage. It was a slow process, moving together inside of a magic bubble. Goblins repeatedly rushed the orb only to be skewered by GOBSlayer, seared by Trinn's fire, or simply flattened by colliding with the seemingly impenetrable sphere Elbore had generated. By the time they reached the elevator and pressed the call button, the goblin onslaught had diminished, and Kalum was nearly completely spent. His body ached, his blood raced, and he couldn't gain control of his breathing. Biomech carcasses lay strewn in smoldering heaps all up and down the corridor. The three of them entered the lift and Elbore released his spell and the shield vanished.

Before keying the button for the fourteenth floor, Kalum eyed Elbore suspiciously. He wasn't about to reveal the location of their room to the man who'd informed Borlan of their presence. "It's okay, Kalum," Trinn said. "He's a friend."

Kalum was about to protest that they all had thought him a friend before, when Elbore shook his head. "No, it's all right," he said to Trinn. "I wouldn't trust me either. Just let me out in the lobby and I'll trouble you no further."

Kalum pressed the button marked L and the lift began its descent.

"How will you reach Rhastor?" Trinn asked Elbore.

The old man sighed. "I may never reach Rhastor. But I'll spend the rest of my life trying."

Kalum took the man's hand, and Trinn hugged him gently. "Thank you for your help, Elbore," she said. "I hope you find your family alive and well."

Elbore smiled at her. "Remember what I told you, Trinn Shadowmoon. Show them."

As the lift door opened and Elbore left them, Kalum couldn't help thinking it wouldn't be the last time they would meet.

TWENTY THREE

A NIGHT NOT RESTED

JUST BEFORE SUNRISE the next morning, the day before the tournament, Borlan awoke to a horrible sound. Freedling was sitting on the floor with the king's head in his lap, tapping him on the forehead with one finger. "Wake up, Your Majesty. Wake up," the man repeated.

"What the hell is going on?" Borlan said, sitting up.

"I couldn't find you, sir," Freedling explained. "You didn't check in at your scheduled bedtime. I searched high and low and finally found you asleep in here on the floor."

"Where's Elbore?" Borlan said, looking around the room. "Where's the woman?"

"They've escaped, Your Majesty."

"Escaped?" Borlan got himself to his feet.

"Yes, Your Majesty. I think you ought to prepare yourself."

"What are you talking about?" Borlan said, growing irritated.

"There was a struggle."

Borlan looked at the door. "Oh no." He rushed through the door and into the hall.

"Wait," Freedling yelled after him. "Your Majesty!"

The corridor was nearly black from smoke and fire. Goblins lay piled on top of one another the entire length of the passage, some of them still smoldering.

"A struggle?" Borlan yelled. "You call this a struggle?"

"I'm sorry, Your Majesty," Freedling said, stepping into the corridor. "Perhaps a bit more than a struggle."

"How?"

"Kalum Tinbrook, Your Majesty. We have photos that were broadcast from the goblins. He was quite thorough."

"What about the upgrades?" Borland asked. "Why didn't they work?"

"Puxley reports that the goblins are working perfectly, Your Majesty. Many of them initiated the new software, but none were able to complete the sequence before being destroyed. Puxley tells me it can take up to ten seconds to complete the process."

Borlan threw his hands in the air. "Unacceptable," he shouted. "I'm surrounded by incompetence." He turned in place, looking in exasperation at the destruction. "They took Elbore?"

"It appears that Elbore went with them willingly, sir," Freedling said in an apologetic tone. "Even helped them."

Borlan heard his blood pulsing in his ears. He shouted at Freedling, "He helped them?"

"It appears so, sir."

"I've had enough of this." Borlan stomped his foot. "This is all Rothburn's doing. Assemble an army of goblins, Freedling. Rebellion or no, we're taking Lenshire—by force!"

Kalum sat bedside as Trinn slept, where he'd stayed all night. He stroked her hair gently. Dark rings had formed beneath her eyes, and her nose was bright red and swollen. When they'd returned to the suite, Blemm had rushed out, returning a short while later with a particularly messy glob of mud that he spread over Trinn's burnt hand. Apparently, as he'd later told it, he'd barged into the Tower's kitchen and stolen honey and wine to mix into the mud, a concoction he'd learned as a child who liked to play with fire.

Kalum had eyed the sticky mixture with skepticism and looked at Hack for help. Hack had simply shrugged and whispered to Kalum, "It's as good a salve as any I could have made." After he'd applied the mud, Blemm wrapped her hand in cloth torn from a room towel.

Sunlight was just beginning to glow against the window and Kalum yawned wearily. "I'm sorry this happened, Trinn," he said to her. Once again, memories of their past adventures sifted through his mind.

This was the part he hated most. Putting his friends in danger had always been difficult for him. Perhaps he'd grown to care too much for his companions. And yet, there was nobody else in the world he'd rather have with him on a quest. Trinn's magic had already proven invaluable on this job; Hack's abilities with computers and Blemm's brute strength and steady course had always been key to their successes. But the risks they took sometimes seemed too much. It was especially hard with Trinn somehow. He had truly feared he'd lost her. What would he have done if she'd been killed?

He thought of Skinner and his dogged pursuit. "I don't know how he keeps finding you." Trinn slept soundly, quietly snoring, but it felt right talking to her. "Hack said he's tracking you. But we don't know how." It didn't make sense. A tracking device would have had to have been on her clothing for Skinner to trace her so accurately to the tower landing. He'd also tracked her to the tavern, but she hadn't been wearing the same clothes that night.

He checked her hand. Blemm's muddy treatment was holding well. "You'll have one hell of a scar," he said. "If it bothers you, maybe you can cover it with a glove or a tattoo." He stood and looked down at her. She was in bad shape but still just as beautiful. "You could even tattoo that crazy design that's on that pendant you wear all the time." An idea snapped in his mind. He reached down to Trinn's neck and took the pendant in his hand. He felt it immediately. It was thin and pliable, a round disk the size of a fingertip stuck firmly to the backside of the pendant. He peeled it off and examined it. He could see tiny wires inside of the translucent material. He'd have to show this to Hack.

Kalum left Trinn to sleep and went out to the main room of the suite.

"Damn it!" It was Hack. Kalum was surprised to find the small man awake and crouched over the computer.

"Don't you ever need sleep?" Kalum asked.

"I slept a couple hours," Hack replied, not looking away from the screen.

"Me too." Kalum yawned and sat on the couch.

"I've been trying to send a message to a colleague of mine, but I can't seem to get access outside of the tower. Something must be wrong with their network."

"But you still have access within?"

Hack nodded. "Yes. Everything. Pretty interesting about that thirteenth floor, huh?"

"Yeah," Kalum said. "What was that all about, anyway?"

"Story goes," Hack turned in his chair, "they simply renumbered the floors to exclude unlucky thirteen. But apparently, they just turned thirteen into a secret floor that can only be accessed by the privileged few." He put a finger beside his nose with a wink. "So don't tell anyone."

"How did you figure it out?"

"I didn't," Hack sighed. "At least, not until it was almost too late. Our suite has no balcony, but since all the odd numbered floors *do* have them, we're obviously on an even floor, which means we couldn't possibly be on thirteen."

Kalum nodded. "I guess that makes sense. Anything else?"

"Yes," Hack said. "Take a look at this." He leaned back from the screen. "I've been going over the video of your goblin massacre last night and I think I found something."

Kalum got back up and leaned over Hack's shoulder to see.

"See? It's only for a couple of frames and it's pretty fuzzy, but right... there! See it?"

Kalum nodded. It looked like a door, but it was slightly recessed and there was no door handle. Looking closely, he could see a small square panel on the wall beside it. A palm scanner.

"I'm thinking that's got to be the mysterious elevator that goes to the penthouse," Hack said, pointing at the image. "I mean, if you're going to have a secret elevator, you'd probably put it on the secret floor, right?"

Kalum nodded. "You could be right."

Hack clapped his hands together. "Then, I think we're ready."

"What do you make of the goblins' eyes turning green?" Kalum asked.

Hack sighed heavily. "I'm not sure. It must be something to do with those goblin upgrades I mentioned before. I didn't notice anything odd, though."

"Neither did I," Kalum said. "But I did my best to take them out as soon as I saw them, just in case it was something really bad."

Hack shrugged. "I guess we won't know until we see it. That's if it's something we can see. Could just be some new type of transmission or a distress call."

"Maybe," Kalum said. "I don't like it. It's all very odd."

"Speaking of odd." Hack turned away from his computer screen and looked with seriousness at Kalum. "We need to talk."

Kalum sat down on the couch. "All right. What's on your mind?"

"Tell me what the hell is going on with you," Hack blurted.

"What do you mean?"

"First you throw a tantrum because I bought a few disruptor grenades, something that could literally save our butts. And then you try and get yourself killed by taking on ten million goblins at once, all the while carrying a grenade on your belt. So, what's going on, Kalum? Are you showing off? Are you trying to prove something? Or are you really trying to kill yourself?"

Kalum shook his head. "Quite the opposite. I'm actually doing everything I can to keep myself, all of us, alive." He undid a few buttons on his tunic and pulled away the fabric, revealing a large thick scar down his chest.

"What the!" Hack came closer, examining the scar. "What happened to you?"

"It was five years ago," Kalum began. "Shortly after we all went our own ways and Mariah and I broke up, I was ambushed and captured by slavers."

"Slavers?"

Kalum nodded. "They took me south to Shadow Glen and forced me to fight in the Fire Trials."

"Gods," Hack gasped. "You were a protector?"

"Yes," Kalum said. "Until I took a goblin sword in the chest."

"Wait," Hack held up a hand. "You were stabbed in the chest? Are you suggesting that you really are GolaStap? The actual Goblin Slayer?"

"That's what they called me. But it's not the point."

"Holy goblin butts! I can't believe this." Hack was on his feet, practically dancing around the room. "I knew it. I knew it! It had to be you. It had to be!"

"Hack. Listen to me," Kalum couldn't help grinning at the little man's exuberance. Hack came back to his seat.

"Sorry, Kalum. Go ahead."

"When I was stabbed, my heart was damaged. It very nearly killed me. They kept me alive with magic, but my heart was too weak." He lowered his head, ashamed of his next words. "They put a reactor inside of me." He looked up at Hack, tears brimming. "A damn goblin reactor, to keep my heart going."

"Gods." Hack's eyes were wide. "Kalum, I'm so sorry. That's why—"

"That's why I can't be near a disruptor grenade when it goes off. Even GOBSlayer triggers a jolt when I use it."

"Why?" Hack said. "I mean, why did they go to such lengths to save you?"

Kalum shook his head. "They didn't want to lose a crowd favorite. I brought people to the games, and they were afraid to lose that. But even with the reactor, I was too weak to continue."

"They set you free?" Hack said.

Kalum nodded. "Yes. They figured I'd earned them enough money to buy my freedom. I've spent the past years working hard to rebuild my strength, but I still have a ways to go."

They sat in silence for some time. Kalum felt like a weight had been lifted from his shoulders. It was a great relief to finally share his story with someone. He knew Hack would respect his privacy but also fully appreciate the technological conundrum he was in.

"It's been five years," Hack said. "Maybe your heart has healed enough to work on its own."

Kalum shrugged. "I've thought of that too, but the only way to find out is to cut me open again and take the damn thing out. Then see if I die or not."

Hack shook his head. "I wish you had told me all this earlier. I can fine-tune GOBSlayer to lessen the impact you've been feeling. That's got to be painful."

"I should have told you," Kalum agreed. "But a good opportunity just never arose to admit that I'm part goblin."

Hack laughed.

"Oh, I almost forgot," Kalum said, eager to change the subject. "I found something I want to show you." He gave Hack the item he'd found attached to Trinn's pendant.

"It's definitely a tracking device," Hack said with assuredness.

"Can you use it to find Skinner?" Kalum asked.

"Well, trackers don't work in both directions," Hack said. Then, with a devilish grin, he said, "But that doesn't mean it can't be of use." He looked up suddenly, and Kalum followed his gaze.

Trinn stood in the doorway to the bedroom, rubbing sleep from her eyes "If you're talking about getting Skinner, count me in," she said.

TWENTY FOUR

TURNING THE TABLES

"YOUR MAJESTY," FREEDLING said from the back of the room. Borlan stood in front of a mirror, primping himself for his coming breakfast with Mariah.

"I'm busy, Freedling."

"Of course you are, sir, but this is of utmost importance."

Borlan sighed. "What is it?"

"I attempted to secure an assault force of goblins, as you requested—"

"I get the feeling I'm not going to like that word, 'attempted.'"

"That's just it, sir." Freedling wrung his hands together. "They're offline."

Borlan turned. "What do mean, offline?"

"I mean, every goblin outside of the city is no longer accepting commands."

"Not accepting commands?" Borlan yelled. "Then what are they doing?"

"Walking, sir."

"Freedling," Borlan gritted his teeth. "If I have to prompt you for every detail this is going to take all day. Just tell me what the hell is going on."

"I'm sorry, but I don't really know, sir."

"Then find me someone who does!" Borlan screamed.

Freedling thought on that for a split second. "Puxley."

John Skinner stood with Torpid Finn, the latest henchman he'd hired to assist him. When the door opened, they stepped out of the lift and into the basement level of Lorr Tower. Torpid was a half-dwarf, shorter than your average human but broad-shouldered and strong. His brown beard covered most of his face, and his mouth only became visible when he spoke, which was something he rarely did.

Skinner checked the tracking device and pointed to the left. "She's still in the vault," he said, noticing a goblin approaching from that direction. He smiled. This Trinn Shadowmoon was turning out to be a lucrative source of income all by herself. He'd already collected the bounty for catching her once. And now that Borlan had foolishly let her escape, the opportunity for an even larger reward had presented itself. If she kept managing to escape from the king's clutches, he could make a fine career of this.

Torpid nodded and they wordlessly set off down the corridor. The goblin held up a hand as they neared, and its yellow eyes scanned over their faces. *<John Skinner,>* its mechanized voice said. *<Do you have a purpose here?>*

Skinner slowed but didn't stop, knowing he had been given security access to the entire tower by Borlan himself. "Yes. We're just checking out the vault area."

<The vault is undergoing maintenance at this time,> the goblin said, but he allowed them to continue. Skinner nodded. *Maintenance.* Certainly, whatever maintenance was being performed had more to do with robbing the tower than any actual repairs.

He glanced at Torpid walking briskly beside him. The half-dwarf carried a large axe with confidence, a weapon that would become useful if Trinn was in the company of one or more of her companions. "You don't talk much, do you?" Skinner asked.

Torpid turned his head and looked at him, his beady eyes darting nervously above his great forest of beard. He said nothing. Skinner nodded. Good. Less talk, more action. That's what was needed anyhow. He glanced again at the tracker and held up a hand for Torpid to stop. Pointing at the wide doorway in front of them to the right, they slowly crept forward.

Peeking around the corner, Skinner spied what he'd hoped for. The heavy vault door was wide open. A light shone from inside the vault. The woman, Trinn, and a pair of her companions were just stepping back inside. The timing was perfect. The close quarters in the vault would make it easier to take control of the situation, but they would need to act quickly. If any one of them came out it would mean splitting up and fighting two separate battles.

He looked at Torpid and whispered almost silently, "On three, we charge. Take out the woman first, do you hear me?" He pulled out his short sword and, holding up three fingers with his other hand, he counted down, "One, two, three!"

He and Torpid rushed ahead. Skinner held his sword pointed forward while Torpid's axe was cocked over one shoulder, ready. They charged into the vault and… nobody. The vault was empty, save for some stacks of cans on the shelves and a couple of wooden barrels. There came a loud and strained yell, startling them both.

"Oh, damn." Skinner realized too late their mistake. The enormous door came crashing closed behind them.

Hack smiled at Blemm as he spun the handle, locking Skinner and the other inside the vault. "That worked rather nicely."

"I was afraid we'd have to wait behind that door all day."

"How do you manage to create three separate illusions?" Hack turned and asked.

Trinn came forward from where she'd been hiding. "It was just one illusion," she said. "It was just of three people. It takes more concentration, but it's not much different from making, say a dog, and keeping its tail wagging while its head is panting."

Blemm nodded at Hack. "I've seen her create a crowd of a

dozen people at once. It's truly amazing."

Hack placed his datapad on the vault door and pressed a button. The screen displayed an x-ray detail of the lock's inner workings.

"What are you doing there?" Trinn asked.

"Just checking that this door actually locks," Hack said. "It's been out of commission for a long time."

Blemm grinned. "I'm guessing that's not a standard feature on all datapads."

Hack winked. "It comes in handy in my line of work."

Trinn put a hand on the door. "So, how long can we keep them in there?" she asked.

Hack keyed up the tower's schedule. "I'll just update the status," he said, trying not to giggle. "There. As of now, this vault is out of commission. I'll schedule further maintenance to occur in... let's say, two weeks."

Blemm laughed. "A fine idea."

"I don't want them to starve to death," Trinn said. "Just keep them out of the way for a while."

"Not to worry," Hack replied. "Since the kitchen has been using this vault for storage, there's plenty of food and drink in there to keep them alive. Plus, it's ventilated, so they sadly won't suffocate."

Trinn nodded. "Two weeks it is then."

Blemm stifled a laugh. "I imagine it's going to get awfully smelly in there. They don't have the luxury of indoor plumbing."

As the three made their way back to the elevator, Trinn remarked, "I haven't told you guys, it's really wonderful being together with you again. I've missed you so much."

"We make a fine team," Blemm said, a tight smile on his lips.

"The mind, the muscle, and the magic." Trinn patted Blemm on the shoulder.

"But then," Hack looked up, "what does that make Kalum?"

"He's a mix of all of us, I think," Blemm answered.

"No," Trinn said, clutching her hands together. "Kalum is definitely the heart."

TWENTY FIVE

RHAST REPOSSESSION

PUXLEY STARED WIDE-EYED at the goblin that pressed a plasma lance to his neck. King Borlan stood with the man, Freedling, an angry sneer on his face. "I'm sorry, Your Majesty," Puxley said. "The order came directly from the Rhast High Command."

"And what *was* this order, exactly?" Borlan asked.

"To issue a broad, kingdom-wide command to every goblin outside of Central City to relocate to a particular set of coordinates."

"Why?" Borlan slammed a fist onto the table.

"For their immediate extraction back to Rhastor, Your Majesty."

Borlan wiped a hand over his eyes. "I don't believe this. You get a little behind on a couple of payments and they repossess your goblins."

"Why did they leave the goblins in Central City?"

"Well," Puxley said, squirming before the goblin's lance. "Two reasons. They didn't want to alert you to the order, and the goblins in the city account for payments already rendered. They're yours to keep."

"Call them back," Borlan demanded. "Rescind the order."

"I can't do that, sir. The command is already in progress. It's being executed as we speak. It's impossible to cancel it now. The goblins will complete the order and then await a new one."

Borlan hit the table again. "Then issue a new order. Tell them to turn around and return to their posts immediately after they've arrived at... wherever they're going."

"Sea View. They're going to Sea View. But I can't do that without approval from Rhast High Command."

"What? You work for me, you idiot," Borlan yelled. "You'll do as I tell you."

"I'm sorry, sir. But the Rhast don't see it that way."

"Well," Borlan spoke calmly now, "the Rhast aren't here with a plasma lance ready to sear your head clean off. So, unless you're prepared to die a most unpleasant death, you'll listen to me. And before you get any noble ideas of sacrificing yourself for your country, you should understand that your family will suffer the same fate."

Puxley nodded. "I'll issue the order."

"No," Borlan shook his head. "I've changed my mind. I have a better idea."

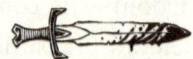

"This is ridiculous," Blemm complained. He and Kalum sat on stools in the fourteenth floor suite. They faced each other as Kalum hacked away at Blemm's beard with a pair of scissors. Piles of Blemm's salt and pepper hair littered the floor around them.

Trinn continued to recover in the next room where Kalum had ordered she rest. She'd argued that she was feeling fine, but Kalum had insisted. She'd already had a rough couple of days and Kalum wanted her as rested as possible for the following day, when she'd really be tested. Hack remained glued to the computer screen, studying the Tower building plans.

"You're the one who said you're tired of being cooped up in here," Kalum said to Blemm. "If you want to go out, you need to be disguised."

"No one knows what I look like."

"We can't be sure of that. Elbore may have given them our descriptions."

"That didn't stop you from obliterating a herd of goblins last night."

Kalum nodded. "You're right. And from now on, I'll need a disguise as well."

"I don't even let my wife touch my beard."

Kalum smiled and continued to cut.

"That was a brave thing you did, by the way," Blemm remarked. "Going to Trinn's rescue."

Kalum shrugged. "She really didn't need rescuing. She and Elbore would have escaped without me." He shook his head. "I was just so worried. It's my worst nightmare."

Blemm nodded knowingly. "Losing Trinn would be a great loss."

"Losing any of you," Kalum admitted. "I just feel responsible. I don't know what I'd do if one of you were killed. It's my worst nightmare."

Blemm's face hardened. "With all due respect. Who the hell do you think you are?"

Kalum looked up, surprised by his friend's reaction.

"We are not your children to be watched over, Kalum." He brushed a hand across his face. "We each entered this coven of our own will. You are not our mother hen, and you are certainly not responsible for our well-being."

Kalum stared at him, letting his words sink in.

"Is that why you left us so suddenly?" Blemm asked. "Why you stopped adventuring?"

"Partly," Kalum said. He resumed shaping the man's rough beard.

Blemm shook his head. "Damn fool."

"Will you stop moving so I can get this even." Another clump of hair the size of a squirrel fell into Blemm's lap.

"If I'm not overstepping the bounds of our friendship," Blemm said, "might I ask what your intentions are with Lady Mariah?"

Kalum stopped cutting. "My intentions?"

"You have a long history with the lady," Blemm said. "Do you perhaps intend to resume that relationship?"

"Blemm, Mariah is a married woman. I intend to rescue her and collect my payment. That's all."

"Nay, my friend. The lady hath never married."

"What are you talking about? Rothburn arranged for her to marry a healer or someone years ago."

Blemm shrugged. "She refused. She has remained unwed and unattached these many years."

"How do you know all this?"

Blemm sighed. "She came to visit my farm, two autumns ago. She was well. She's made a life for herself as a healer. I'm surprised you know nothing of this."

Kalum shook his head. "I've had no contact with her. Not since…"

"A healer," Blemm said. "Who would believe?"

Memories flooded back into Kalum's mind, those he had pushed away long ago.

Upon his initial return to Lenshire, before the baron had paid him to leave, Kalum had returned to the Rothburn home and came unsuspectingly across Mariah and her father in conversation. He was not normally one to eavesdrop, but Mariah's tone gave him pause, and he listened.

"Regalado won't accept you for study with your current experience," the baron was saying.

"But, Father," Mariah whined. "I've dreamt of becoming a healer since I was a girl. Surely there's something you can do."

"I'm sorry, Mariah. He said he never accepts students without experience, unless there's a healer in the family that can act as a mentor of sorts. And as you know, our family has no history of healers."

"It's ridiculous," Mariah cried. "How can I gain experience if no one will teach me?"

"There may be a way," the baron began. "But no. It's too drastic."

"Please," Mariah said. "Tell me. I'll do anything."

"Jacoby was a student of Regalado's, one of his finest he tells me. If you were to marry him—"

"No, Father," Mariah said.

"He's a fine man, Mariah," her father coaxed, "You know that. He loves you, and he could provide you with so much, including your dream of becoming a healer."

There was a long silence, in which Kalum imagined Mariah glaring at the baron in fury, her mouth pursed shut, as she often did when she was angry. But more quickly than he'd have believed, she answered. "Very well, Father. I'll marry Jacoby."

Blemm sighed heavily, blowing wisps of hair into the air. "I only ask about Mariah because of my concern for Trinnity."

"What has Trinn got to do with it?"

Blemm barked a sharp laugh, showering Kalum in tiny hairs. "For a man of your considerable intelligence, you are truly ignorant in the affairs of a woman's heart, and your own heart, for that matter."

"Trinn and I are friends."

"She loves you."

Kalum shook his head.

"And you love her," Blemm continued. "Don't deny it."

"But…" Kalum's mind spun. Had he really ignored his own feelings for so long?

"You would do well to not complicate the matter with nostalgic fantasies of past loves."

"I have no fantasies of love, past or otherwise."

Blemm nodded. "Very well. Are we done here?"

"We're done."

"How do I look?"

Kalum looked at him, inspecting his work, and then nodded. "It's not too bad, for my first time."

"Gods of mayhem," Blemm stammered. "Fetch me a mirror so that I may assess the damage."

Hack had been paying no attention to the conversation between Kalum and Blemm, his focus being on studying the building plans. He'd gone repeatedly over the footage of Kalum's massacre the night before, and he was certain he'd spotted a vault on the thirteenth floor. From what he could perceive from the jerky video, down a particular side corridor, several goblins stood guard outside the massive door. It had to be the true Tower vault. *That's where I'll find the good stuff,* he thought. Now, he scanned through the tower's plans, studying the maze of ventilation ducts and crawlspaces, seeking the best way to access his new find.

TWENTY SIX

KALUM TINBROOK

MARIAH CHECKED THE clock on the side table yet again. Borlan had not arrived for breakfast as he normally did. She'd grown oddly accustomed to the king's morning visits. They were always the same. In fact, she was counting on similar visits in order to carry out her plans.

It was nearly an hour past their usual time when Borlan finally arrived. He seemed distracted from the moment he entered. "Your breakfast is coming," he said. "But I'm sorry, I won't be joining you this morning. Too much going on."

Mariah nodded. "That's okay." She had hoped to have another opportunity to give the goblin orders, but she didn't want to seem obvious. "Is everything all right?" she asked.

Borlan nodded. "Fine. But before I go, I want to ask you about Kalum Tinbrook."

"Kalum Tinbrook?" Mariah looked up in surprise. "Why would you ask about him?"

Borlan shrugged casually. "I know from your files that you were in a relationship with the man some years ago. Tell me about him. What kind of man was he?"

"What's there to tell? I haven't seen nor spoken to him in years. He was a treasure hunter, and a good one. But I worried for his safety. I always feared he'd be killed on one of his quests."

"So, what happened?"

"It didn't work out," Mariah said. *What is this all about*, she wondered. *What does Kalum have to do with anything?*

"That's interesting," Borlan said, "because I remember Kalum's name from a conversation I had long ago with your father." He watched her, as if expecting a reaction. She forced herself to remain expressionless. "He contacted me some years ago and requested that I apprehend Kalum Tinbrook for crimes against the kingdom. He was desperate to get him away from you."

"My father did that?" Mariah was truly surprised. Her father had been known to act in a lowly manner at times, but she'd no idea he'd tried something like this.

"Oh, yes," Borlan replied. "But the odd part is that I was far too busy negotiating with the Rhast at the time, and when I told him thus, he replied that he would simply have to pay this Kalum off to make him go away."

Mariah held the king's gaze, for he was surely hoping for a reaction of shock or dismay.

"That's right," she replied. "My father was never happy with my relationship with Kalum. He thought him crude, unpolished, and poor. Unfit for the daughter of Baron Rothburn. He went so far as to arrange that I be married to another man. One who could give me everything I wanted."

Borlan looked surprised. "You knew of this? That must have been difficult."

"It should have been. And yet, I accepted the proposal for my own selfish reasons. Kalum learned of all this, somehow. I suspect my father told him. And so you see, it is not that surprising at all that he chose to take my father's money and leave. I don't blame him."

"And so your father forced you to marry a man you didn't love," Borlan said cruelly, seemingly trying to dig at her emotions.

"No," Mariah said flatly. "I might have, for my father told me that only in marriage to this man could I hope to study under Regalado, the Master Healer. But I was accepted under his tutelage anyhow. And do you know why?"

Borlan shook his head.

"Because Kalum went to Regalado after leaving Lenshire and bribed him to accept me as a student. He gave everything that my father had paid him and more from his own coffers, in order that I could fulfill my dream of becoming a healer."

"So that you wouldn't marry another," Borlan said.

Mariah lifted her chin. "No. I only learned of it because Regalado chose to tell me of it when I had completed my studies. It's true that Kalum saved me from having to marry, but he never returned to Lenshire. Why would he? To try and regain the hand of the woman who had betrayed him so? No. He left and I never faulted him for it."

Borlan simply nodded. Mariah knew he'd not gotten the reaction he'd hoped. She could only guess he was trying to turn her against her father.

"So, in answer to your question, Your Majesty," Mariah said. "That's the kind of man that Kalum Tinbrook is."

TWENTY SEVEN

PUXLEY PROBLEMS

PUXLEY SAT AT the bar of the Cut Your Losses Saloon, a dark and quiet watering hole built right within the lobby of Lorr Tower, and firmly banged his head against the datapad in front of him. A mug of mulled wine, his fifth to his recollection, sat beside the pad, and he took another deep gulp. He was reeling from the intoxicating effects of the drink, but his mood was none improved. What a horrible day.

Having fulfilled Borlan's demands, under threat of death, and updated the goblins' programing, he'd been swiftly removed and locked out of the Biomech Control Center, for fear that he'd try to undo the damage he'd been forced to inflict. He'd argued with Borlan that his plans were dangerous, not only to the Rhast, but to the entire Lorrean kingdom. But Borlan, bent on revenge, simply wouldn't listen. The Rhast had bruised the king's ego, but even more, they'd hurt his feelings, and Borlan was only capable of responding with the attitude of a spoiled child. *They hurt me. So I'll hurt them back.*

For the past several hours, he'd tried in vain to access the control center through his datapad. He was still able to view the Tower network and the day-to-day workings of the hotel staff. A lot of good that did him, since all of his access points to the control center and the biomechs had been deleted. In essence, he was completely cut off. Now everything was ruined. How could he fix this? There just seemed no way. In despair, he banged his head again on the pad.

"You look like a man who's had a bad day."

Puxley looked up. A large man with a roughly hewn beard was seating himself on a barstool at the end of the bar. Though he was cast in shadows, Puxley could see that he was dressed in strangely mismatched clothes, as though he'd dressed in the dark. Puxley simply nodded at the man in greeting. He wasn't in much mood for conversation.

"No luck at the tables?" the man asked.

Puxley sighed. There seemed no option but to talk to this stranger. "I don't gamble," he said. "But yes, it's been a manure pile of a bad day." Puxley squinted, trying to focus his bleary eyesight. The man seemed familiar somehow; something about his eyes. But he couldn't place him.

"Well, I doubt it could be as bad as all that," the man said.

"Oh, really?" Puxley grinned. "You have no idea."

"Well, if you want to get it off your shoulders, I'm here to listen." The stranger ordered a mug of mead from the bartender and left Puxley to his misery. Puxley glanced again at him. He'd definitely seen him before.

"Fine," Puxley shouted, not meaning for his words to come so loudly. "I'll tell you." He wiped his sleeve across his nose and began. "King Borlan is a bumbling psychopath."

"Good Gods," the bearded man hissed. He wasn't even paying attention. He was staring out into the Tower lobby. "Excuse me, friend," the man muttered and left the bar, leaving his drink, and Puxley, behind.

Well, that's just terrific, Puxley thought. *One more fine addition to the manure pile.* Gulping down the remainder of his drink, he slammed his cup onto the bar. "Bartender," he called. "Let's have another..." He blinked. It came to him slowly, but it came. A day earlier, King Borlan, the obnoxious ass, had instructed him to research Kalum Tinbrook and all of his companions. Puxley had spent hours poring over photos and stories on the net. Kalum's oldest friend and longtime companion was a man called Blemm, a potato farmer, but also a competent warrior. Puxley blinked again. The man he'd just been talking to, the one who'd offered to listen to Puxley's woes, it was Blemm. His beard was shorter, but it was Blemm. He'd bet his life on it. Puxley slammed a game chip down on the bar as payment and rushed out into the lobby. He looked all around, searching for the man. Blemm could lead him to Kalum Tinbrook, and Kalum Tinbrook would lead him to...

TWENTY EIGHT

NOBBY NEGOTIATIONS

B LEMM MADE HIS way through the crowded lobby, keeping
a close eye on the woman he'd just spotted from the bar. She
was walking with, or rather being escorted by, two men. He was
just able to keep track of the men over the crowd. The woman
was impossible to see, for she was only three feet tall. It was
Katriana, Baron Rothburn's halfling, um…nobby, bodyguard.

The two men exited the lobby through a side door,
presumably with Katriana. Blemm stopped at the door. There
was a palm scanner beside it and a small sign that read: Tower
Personnel Only. No way to get through without making a
scene. What was the nobby doing here? Why was she with
Tower employees? Blemm looked all about, searching for
answers, possibilities, what to do. He spotted a bank of public
comm stations. Perfect.

Katriana was led along a narrow corridor and into a small
conference room. The red-haired man asked for her weapons,
and she surrendered the two hand axes she always carried. He
set the weapons on a small counter by the door and stood close
by, as if on guard. The other, a narrow dark-haired man with
eyeglasses, introduced himself as Freedling and told her that
the king would be joining them shortly.

Katriana cleared her throat and nodded. She was admittedly
nervous to be meeting with the king of Lorr, but this was her

assignment. After receiving word that the rescue attempt by Kalum Tinbrook and his companions had failed, Baron Rothburn was left with no choice but to draw up contracts that relinquished all rights and titles to the land of Lenshire in return for his daughter's safe return. Katriana was here to finalize those contracts and complete the transaction. She keyed on her datapad and was just opening the first contract when a door at the back of the room opened and in walked King Borlan.

Katriana felt a wave of relief fall over her when she saw him. He was nothing to be intimidated by. Skinny and frail, his anxious eyes betrayed his nervousness and fear. But his pointy chin raised high, and his narrow mouth pursed tight, revealed his pomposity. *This is a man who can be manipulated,* Katriana thought. *This is a man guided by his own ego.*

"Well," Borlan said with an arrogant grin on his face. "I'm pleased that Rothburn has finally come to his senses."

"You forced his hand. What choice does he have?"

Borlan sat across the table from her and Freedling took a chair beside him. "It's unfortunate that the baron chose to attempt a rescue instead of complying with my offer," Borlan went on. "So many lives wasted. But, I suppose that's the cost of doing business."

"To be clear," Katriana said. "The baron does not view this as a business transaction. This is extortion, plain and simple." She forced herself to be blunt, to throw the king off his game. It worked.

The king bristled visibly. "Whatever you choose to call it is insignificant," he stammered. "What's important is the safety of the lady, Mariah. Now, I presume the contracts are in order. Let's get on with it."

Katriana keyed her pad to open the first of the many forms to be signed. Before the document could open, however, a message window popped up on her screen:

INCOMING PUBLIC CALL FROM: [BLEMM]

She stared at the screen in confusion. How could Blemm

be calling her? According to Borlan, Blemm and the rest of the rescue team were dead.

Thinking fast, she picked up the datapad and stood. "Is there someplace that I can take a private communication?" she asked. "The baron is calling, regarding our transaction."

Borlan stared at her for several seconds. "Is that so?" he said before nodding to the red-haired man who stood at the entrance. The man returned a nod and opened the door, saying, "This way, miss."

Katriana hurried out with the man, who led her to an adjacent room. The room was empty but for a small table and four chairs. "I'll be right outside when you're finished," the man told her and left, closing the door behind him.

Katriana quickly keyed the message to accept the incoming call. A video image of Blemm opened. "How are you alive?" she said. "And oh, Gods! What did you do to your beard?"

"What are you doing in Central City?" Blemm demanded. "Who are you meeting with?"

Katriana explained to Blemm that they had received word that the rescue had failed and all were dead.

"We tried to contact you, but communication was blocked for some reason."

"Yes, all comm traffic in or out of the tower has been blocked."

"Well, when the baron couldn't reach you, he assumed you were dead."

"That's ridiculous," Blemm roared. "No one is dead. Well, except maybe a hundred or so goblins. The rescue is still planned for tomorrow morning. Don't sign anything with Borlan."

"We're already in a meeting," Katriana said. "If I back out now he'll know something is up."

"You're just going to have to think of something."

She rolled her eyes. "You're a big help."

"Just get out of there. I'll meet you in the lobby."

When Katriana was led back into the meeting, Borlan

was impatiently drumming his fingers on the table. "I trust everything is in order," he said with a withering stare.

"Actually," Katriana said, steeling her nerves. "There appears to be a problem with the contract. The one I have here is an old version, and the baron will be sending the new one shortly. Perhaps it's best that we meet again, in say, one hour?" She turned to the counter to collect her weapons.

"No," the king said, evil in his eyes. "That's unacceptable."

Katriana took a deep breath and turned to face him. "I apologize for the delay, Your Majesty. But it can't be helped."

"I happen to know that you did not receive a communication from Rothburn," Borlan growled. "Because right now all communications in and out of this building are blocked."

Katriana gave a nervous laugh. "That can't be true, because the baron just..."

"I don't know what you're up to," Borlan said, "but I suggest you sit back down and produce that contract or you will be joining Mariah today... in death."

Katriana swallowed nervously. The situation had taken a dangerous turn and she feared she would have to fight her way out. No matter. She'd fought her way out of worse situations before. She noted the position of the man standing guard and of her axes on the counter.

"I assure you, Your Majesty," she said, taking a step backward toward the counter. "If you'll just allow me to get a message to the baron, we can work all of this out."

"I don't want your assuredness. I want that contract."

It was time. Katriana spun around, leaping onto the counter where her weapons lay. With a flick, she flung one of the axes at the red-haired man, who was rushing to grab her. It struck him in his torso and he froze in shock. Katriana flexed her gloved fist quickly closed twice, then open again, triggering the axe she'd thrown to dislodge itself and fly back into her grip. The wounded man clutched a hand to his bleeding chest, eyes wide in shock. It was a fair wound, but he'd survive. Holding the axes aggressively, she faced the king and the terror-struck Freedling. "You've been very rude," she said. "I'm leaving now."

The two men, their eyes wide with fear, nodded their heads, short and quick. Katriana jumped from the counter and, stuffing her datapad under one arm, dashed from the room.

Puxley had followed Blemm through the Lorr Tower lobby, keeping his distance so not to be seen. The big man had seemed to examine one of the back-of-house doorways before making his way to a public comm station. Puxley leaned against a pillar and kept close watch. Once Blemm had finished his call, he returned to the door and waited. What was he up to? Puxley wondered. Within a couple of minutes, the door flew open and a tiny woman ran out. She and Blemm made hurried conversation and then ran, ducking into a crowd of people waiting to check in for the tournament, and then they pushed their way toward the elevators. Seconds later, a pair of goblins exited the same door the woman had come through. They looked about, appearing to search for the woman.

Puxley rushed to keep up with Blemm and his new companion, but he reached the elevators just as the door closed with the two inside. Quickly, he pulled open his datapad and accessed the tower's Elevator Control Application. The ECA showed him the status and location of all the elevators. The lift that carried Blemm and the woman stopped at the fourteenth floor, a floor currently closed for remodeling. Interesting.

When Blemm returned to the suite with Katriana, there was much discussion about what had happened. Everyone was relieved that she had escaped before turning over Lenshire to Borlan.

"When you return to Lenshire, tell the baron that all is well," said Kalum. "We'll retrieve Mariah tomorrow and return her to him shortly after."

"I'll send him a message," Katriana replied. "But I'm not going anywhere until *we* have rescued Mariah."

"We?"

Katriana nodded. "Borlan really pissed me off. So unless you think I'll be in the way, I'm joining the team."

Kalum looked at the others for objections.

"Look at her," Hack grinned. "She certainly won't be in the way."

"You can fight?" Kalum asked, eyeing the axes at her waist.

"Of course I can fight."

Hack stepped closer, staring hard at the nobby's weapons. "Are those…?"

"Auto-retrievable?" Katriana said. "Yes, they are. The handles are sub-remotely linked to sensors in my gloves."

"Cool," he whispered, his eyes wide. "Can I see?"

Katriana pulled one of the axes from her belt and threw it hard across the room, where it stuck firmly into the portrait of Borlan, splitting his forehead. Then with a flick of her hand, the ax whistled back through the air and into her grip.

Hack smiled. "Cool," He said again.

"You're in," Kalum said.

PART THREE

GOBLIN GAMBIT

TWENTY NINE

AN UNDERHANDED UNDERTAKING

THAT NIGHT THEY all turned in early, wanting to be well-rested for the next morning's rescue. Katriana shared Trinn's room, while Kalum shared the other room with the roaring snoring Blemm. Only Hack remained awake as he secretly prepared to carry out his plan, that being to rob the thirteenth floor vault.

While he couldn't be positive the vault held anything of tremendous value, his principles as a thief would not allow him to walk away without at least trying. The basement vault, his original target, had been a bust, but he felt confident that this vault, tucked away on a hidden floor, would provide ample spoils. And if not, the act of penetrating King Borlan's secret tower vault was enough to sustain him for years within the thieves' guild just on bragging rights alone.

Having lived a life of less than honorable deeds, Hack had never been prone to the qualms of his actions. And yet tonight, there persisted a guilty prod in his gut from deceiving Kalum's demand that he wait until after their current job. But Hack rationalized that the chaos that would surely ensue after the robbery would provide additional distraction from the rescue. Plus, the treasure he hoped to gain would be sufficient recompense for his blatant defiance.

He'd done his research and acquired the tools he needed. It was time. Crouched low behind the sofa, he quietly removed the screws to the floor grate that provided fresh air to the suite. In his extensive research of the tower, he'd discovered that the network of air ducts that ran throughout the complex was... extensive. Conditioning the air was a new concept in the kingdom, provided by the Rhast of course. The air ducts were just large enough that he could wiggle his way through them to a ceiling access on the floor below, one very close to the vault. Reaching the vault in this manner would reduce the length of hallway he'd have to traverse and diminish the risk of bumping into the chance goblin.

Luckily, everyone had become accustomed to the noise of Blemm's outrageous snoring, and so the quiet racket of Hack's work went unnoticed. Everyone, that is, except the nobby, Katriana, who found it nearly impossible to sleep. Annoyed and restless, she got up to find something to stuff in her ears.

"What do you think you're doing?" Katriana asked, having just walked in on Hack attempting to squirm his way into an open floor vent.

Hack looked up in surprise. "Be quiet," he whispered. "I'm not doing anything. Why are you out of bed? Go back to sleep."

"Don't talk to me like I'm a child."

Hack grinned. "If the tiny shoe fits."

"Tell me what you're up to, or I'll scream."

"Go ahead," Hack dared her. "Who would hear you over Blemm's snoring?"

"Is that snoring?" Katriana asked. "I thought someone was neutering a bear."

Hack couldn't help laughing. "Okay, I'll tell you." He explained as succinctly as possible his plan to rob the thirteenth floor vault.

"Sounds dangerous," Katriana said. "I'm going with you."

"I don't have time to argue with you," Hack said. "You can't go."

"I *am* going," Katriana said. "You need someone to watch your back."

"If things go as planned, I won't need my back watched."

"And if they don't?"

Hack seemed to think on that for a few seconds. "Fine," he said.

"Good." Katriana nodded and turned away. "I'll grab my axes. This should be fun."

Within minutes, the two were squirming their way through the narrow ducts. Even for a small man, Hack struggled to push his way along, and he was beginning to wonder if using the elevator might not have been a better idea. Having studied the layout, he slowly led the way. Everything he needed he had in his new blue bag tied firmly at his waist.

"Can't you move any faster?" Katriana quietly complained behind him.

"I'm sure this is like a grand corridor to a nobby," Hack replied. "But it's pretty damn tight for me."

"Probably doesn't help that you're wearing coveralls four sizes too big."

"It's a maintenance uniform. There weren't a lot of size options when I stole it."

The remainder of the journey was quiet, and soon they'd lowered themselves into an unoccupied office on the thirteenth floor.

"Now, when we get to the vault let me do the talking," Hack told Katriana as he pulled a metal contraption from the bag. "And hide those axes someplace."

The nobby untucked her shirt and let it hang over her weapons, and they exited the room into the corridor. They only had to round one corner to reach the vault area where a pair of goblins stood motionless by the heavy door. One of them turned its glowing eyes on Hack.

<This is a restricted area. Are you required to be here?>

Hack held up the contraption. "We're supposed to install a new time lock. It's on the schedule."

The goblin's eyes flickered as it presumably verified the maintenance schedule that Hack had already modified.

<Very well,> its mechanical voice grated. <You are authorized. The halfling is not.>

"Who are you calling halfling, frog face?" Katriana barked.

"This is Penelope Hightower," Hack said, raising his voice. "She's the lead engineer at Mage Industries, the company that makes this lock." He held the lock up in the goblin's face. "She's here to insure proper installation and accurate calibration in order to meet specification. So, unless *you* know a thing or two about precision electronic vault security equipment, I need her to be here."

The goblin held up a hand. <*Very well. Request granted. She's your responsibility. Go ahead.*>

"Thank you, officer," Hack said and moved to the door. From his bag, he brought out the thermic bore and affixed it to the tripod. After a quick measurement, he lined up the bore to a specific spot on the vault door. Glancing at the goblin that he'd spoken to before, he said, "You probably don't want to be around for this. These can have a negative effect on obsolete equipment, like yourselves."

The goblin looked at him momentarily, its eyes flickering, then nodded. <*GOB-126, Let's go.*>

The creatures walked away, leaving Hack and Katriana alone with the vault.

"I thought they'd never leave," Hack said.

"You do have a way with goblins," she replied.

Hack shrugged. "Biomechs like situations to be simple and binary. Yes or no. They're easily baffled by complicated explanations and subtle insults. Don't look directly at the beam."

Once Katriana had turned away, Hack pulled on his goggles and switched on the bore. A red beam fired from the bore, melting a deepening hole in the door. Smoke rose from the spot, and Hack felt the heat of the laser on his face as the steel around the hole began to glow orange.

"What is that thing?" Katrina asked.

"It's a thermic bore. It's used for mining ore."

"What's it doing?"

"I need to disable the door's actual time lock before I can open the door. If I've lined it up correctly, the bore should destroy the lock shortly. Just a few more seconds." He smiled at her. "This is going better than I expected."

GOB-180 stood guard at its new location precisely forty-one feet from the vault door, its processor clicking away. Something about the vault maintenance worker had triggered an error in its equivocation circuit.

It turned to its partner, GOB-126. *<Did something seem funny to you about that maintenance guy?>*

GOB-126 blinked its yellow eyes. *<I'm not programmed to understand humor.>*

<Not funny ha ha,> Goblin-180 explained. *<Funny strange.>*

<He was on the schedule.>

<That's true.> GOB-180 nodded and tried to let the matter drop, but his uncertainty chip was stuck in a mistrustfulness loop, which had triggered another error. *<Do you want to contact Security and verify things?>*

<Nope.>

<Well, I'm going to call for verification.>

<Knock yourself out.>

Hack worked quickly. The time lock that prevented the door from being opened, except at certain times, had been destroyed by the thermic bore, and now he simply needed to pick the lock. Holding his datapad against the door, he watched the pins fall into place.

"There," he said, shutting down the pad. "Cross your fingers." He gave the vault handle a turn and heard the joyous sound of the heavy lock disengaging. A wide smile stretched across his face. "Perfect."

<Stop what you're doing,> came a goblin voice just as Hack was pulling the door open. He turned to see two red-eyed goblins closing in on them, stun sticks sparking in their hands.

"Is there a problem, officer?" Hack asked, but Katriana was apparently taking no chances and went on the attack. One of the nobby's axes landed deep between the eyes of the first goblin, causing its eyes to go dark. Her second axe grazed off the ear of the other creature and clattered to the floor but then spun around and returned to her grasp as if attached by an elastic band. The goblin with the head wound waved its stun stick as it stepped forward, clearly blinded. The axe must have severed its optical circuit, Hack surmised.

Hack looked about for options. The blinded goblin was less of a threat but still dangerous, since it could still navigate by sound alone. The other goblin side-stepped for position and moved toward Katriana. The woman landed her axe this time over the goblin's left eye, sending sparks shooting. It stopped for a split second, assessing its damage, and then continued its slow charge.

The blind goblin swung its stick wildly, barely missing Hack's shoulder. Hack ducked around the creature and flipped on the switch on the bore. His original intention was to use the device's noise to disorient the goblin, but as the beam lanced into the vault door, an idea came to him. He spun the bore on its tripod and aimed the beam at the goblin that was closing in on Katriana, another axe embedded in its shoulder. The bore's laser hit the creature in the neck, piercing clean through and into the wall beyond.

Startled, the goblin spun around to face the attack, but in its rotation, it allowed the beam from the bore to completely sever its head from its body. The creature collapsed at Katriana's feet, its head bouncing away like a child's lost ball.

Hack spun the beam in the other direction and similarly sliced the top of the blind goblin's head off, just as the creature struck the bore with its stunstick. The bore died a spectacular death as flames and sparks launched in all directions. Now, with both goblins down, Hack pulled again at the vault door.

"More coming," Katriana shouted, her axes back in her grips. "Listen!"

Hack stopped. Sure enough, the sound of heavy, mechanically-paced footsteps were coming from around the corner. Lots of them. He retrieved one of the two-wave Crasher grenades he'd brought along from a pouch on his belt and, pressing the button on its edge, he threw it just as four more goblins rounded the corner.

The grenade clattered to the ground and then detonated in wholly unspectacular fashion. A piercing high-pitched whistle and a series of clicks were all it produced. For a moment Hack's heart sank. Was it a dud? But the next moment, all at once, the goblins toppled to the ground like puppets whose strings had been cut.

"Cool," Hack whispered. Still, the sound of footsteps told him more goblins were approaching. "Come on, quick," he said. "Get inside the vault."

"But we'll be trapped," Katriana argued, rushing in regardless.

"We'll worry about that later," Hack said, following her inside. "Let's just survive the next few seconds, okay?"

Once inside, they both pulled the door closed and Hack flipped the switch for the lights. He spun the interior handle to lock them inside.

"I hope you can get us out of here," Katriana said nervously.

"Of course I can. I did it once, right?" Hack turned toward her.

"Good," she said. "I'm not really comfortable in confined spaces."

Hack stared, wide-eyed. "Gods, I've never seen anything so beautiful."

Katriana ran a tiny hand through her hair and smiled. "Thank you. But aside from this being a really inappropriate time, you're just not my type," she said.

Hack pointed beyond the nobby, and Katriana turned. The back wall of the vault was completely hidden from view by stacks upon stacks of gold coins. They sparkled in the vault's light, the treasure reaching nearly to the ceiling.

Katriana's hands fell to her side. "Oh."

Hack pulled the blue bag from his belt. "Here," he said, tossing the bag to Katriana. "Start filling that up." He pulled out his datapad and began keying in commands. "I need to get a message to the others. I hope I can reach them from in here."

THIRTY

ROBBERY REPERCUSSIONS

KALUM AWOKE WITH a start. Blemm was shaking him and talking in his ear. "Wake up, Kalum. We have to go."

"What's going on?" Kalum asked, suddenly alert.

"Hack's got himself in a mess. We have to go get him."

"Hack?"

Blemm leaned against the bureau and pulled on his boots. "Just got a message. Goblins have him and Katriana trapped in the thirteenth floor vault."

Kalum knew immediately what had happened. Hack had tried to rob the vault. He wasn't surprised; it was in the little man's nature. He'd told Hack repeatedly not to do it while they focused on Mariah, but he hadn't really expected Hack's patience to last. It didn't matter. All that mattered now was to get him out of there alive.

Blemm picked up his hammer and held it above his head in a monstrous stretch. "Guess things are going to get exciting quicker than we thought. Should we wake Trinn?"

Kalum shook his head. "Let her sleep. She needs all the rest she can get for later."

Once the two men were dressed and armed, Kalum went to the desk where Hack had spent the majority of the past few days and retrieved the glove that bore the king's handprint. Beside the computer console sat one of the disruption grenades Hack had purchased, and he stuffed it into a pocket. He hoped he wouldn't have to use it, but if things got really bad, as a last resort, it might just save his friends.

"Are they coming?" Katriana asked.

"They're coming."

"Good. I need to get out of here."

"We'll be out soon."

Hack wiped sweat from his forehead and tried to slow his breathing. Gold was always heavier than he expected.

"Hack."

"What?"

"This was fun."

Blemm saw red. As usually happened in battle, Blemm's adrenaline-fueled rage took over, transforming him into a rampaging animal. He slipped into a nightmare-like state, where slaughter and destruction were paramount. His actions were driven by an unconscious battle-rage that he had little control of. As he fought his way along the corridor, he had the dim awareness of another fighting beside him: a friend. One of the green-skinned creatures managed a lucky jab with its stun stick and an arch of electricity jolted through him. He roared in fury and crushed the ugly beast beneath his hammer. As more and more goblins scurried from doorways and side corridors, their eyes glowing menacingly, Blemm's berserk rampage only intensified. Finally he reached a side enclave, where a crowd of goblins stood massed before a great metal door with their backs turned to him. Easy pickings.

Inside the vault, there came a sound like thunder, as though a blistering storm raged just outside the door. Hack grinned knowingly. "I think our friends have arrived."

"At last," said Katriana, her voice quivering. "Can you open the door now?"

"Sure." He pulled out his datapad. "Give me two minutes."

Kalum stood back and caught his breath. Hack's adjustments to GOBSlayer had worked miracles. No longer did he feel that uncomfortable kick in his chest from the sword's disruptor.

He watched Blemm closely. His red-faced friend stood by the vault door, breathing heavily, his face wet with sweat. As he calmed, the color drained and his eyes became more focused. Slowly, a smile appeared, then a tremendous laugh. "Gods of war! I've missed that," he yelled. "It's been too long." He let his hammer down to his side. "You know, at first I was annoyed with Hack for getting us into this mess, but now I just want to hug him." He laughed again.

Kalum nodded. "I'm so glad you enjoyed it. Are they still inside?"

Blemm looked at the door and shrugged.

As if in answer to Kalum's question, the iron handle spun on its own, and slowly, the great door swung open. Katriana rushed out, clearly happy to be freed. And there stood Hack in the doorway, looking sheepish. He carried at his side a velvety blue bag. "I'm sorry," was all he said.

"We'll talk about it later," Kalum said. "Right now, we have to fight our way back."

At these words, Blemm looked up, his smile widening. "There's more?"

It seemed to Kalum that there was an endless supply of goblins. He led the way back to the elevator, while Blemm mopped away the steady flow of biomechs that came at them from behind. Hack and Katriana stayed between the two warriors, but Katriana's axes flew all about, seeming to ricochet as they struck a goblin, then just as smoothly flew back to her. Once again, the changing eye color of the goblins concerned Kalum. Most glowed red as the goblins signaled for even more reinforcements. While some of the biomechs just entering the fray continued to exhibit the normal yellow-eyed glow, one occasionally came into close quarters, its eyes would change to green. Kalum made an effort to dispatch the green-eyed goblins fast, still not knowing what the color change meant.

Seeing an opening, Kalum shouted for the others to make a run for the lift. Hack and the nobby raced to the elevator, dodging nimbly around another goblin that appeared from the shadows. Kalum looked back and tensed. The number of goblins attacking from Blemm's direction had increased dramatically. The big man swung wildly with his hammer, taking out two, three at a time, but the onslaught looked greater than he would be able to handle for long.

Fearing for his friend's safety, Kalum reached for the disruption grenade but stopped. Blemm seemed to be gaining control of the goblin assault as the growing mass of goblin carcasses blocked the way. He hammered away, roaring in frenzied anger as goblins struggled to climb over the battered bodies of their fallen companions. In a rare moment of lucidity, Blemm turned and yelled at Kalum to run for it. "I'll hold them back," he shouted.

Kalum didn't waste time debating the matter. He ran for the lift, skewering another goblin as he passed. The faster he could get to the elevator, the faster Blemm could retreat from the growing threat surrounding him.

He reached the open lift where Hack and Katriana stood waiting and turned back to the corridor. "Blemm, let's go!" He had no idea if his friend had heard him, for he was deep into whatever battle frenzy tended to overtake him in battle.

A slew of goblins had broken through the bottleneck of wreckage and were beginning to surround Blemm. He took another jolt from a stun stick and howled with rage. Kalum saw a pair of green-eyed goblins move in close. As Blemm raised his hammer into the air, another stun stick hit him in the ribs, and he doubled over from the charge.

His friend was in trouble, Kalum knew. The man had the

strength of a bear, but how many stun strikes could he take? "Stay here," he said to the others and, readying GOBSlayer, he dashed to help Blemm. But just as he stepped from the elevator, an explosion erupted in front of him, the shock blasting him backwards into the lift.

Everything was fuzzy. His ears rang loudly, and he could only barely hear the anguished cry from Hack, "No!" The lift doors began closing, and the last thing Kalum saw was Blemm's crumpled and smoking body lying in the corridor amongst a tangle of burning debris.

THIRTY ONE

DISSENSION AND DESIRE

THE FIRST THOUGHT to enter Kalum's mind when he awoke was that it had been a nightmare. Hack had not robbed Borlan's vault and Blemm had not been killed.

Trinn was sitting on the bed beside him. She looked at him through puffy red eyes, eyes that told him it had been no dream. He put his hands over his face, his thoughts threatening to push him over a cliff of despair. Blemm had been his oldest friend. They'd met when Kalum was barely a man. Blemm had been his brother in countless battles, his confidant in matters of the heart, and his voice of reason when Kalum, as he often did, made things more complicated than they needed to be.

He opened his eyes to Trinn, speaking of complicated. It had been Blemm's opinion that Kalum should finally admit his feelings for Trinn. Well, the old warrior had never been wrong before. What should he say? Something charming.

"Blemm said that you love me."

Trinn's eyes widened and a welcome smile appeared on her face. "Did he?"

"That's what he said." Kalum sat up and faced her. "And he also said I should just admit that I'm in love with you too."

Trinn nodded, ever so slightly. "Well, go ahead."

Kalum stared at her. "Go ahead what?"

"Admit that you're in love with me."

In answer, he kissed her, long and wonderful. But was it right? They were both emotionally wrecked. This is what had happened years before and it had almost ruined their friendship.

"No," he said, pulling away. "First, you have to know this isn't just my grief talking. There are a thousand things I wish I'd have said to Blemm, but now it's too late. I don't want to make the same mistake with you. Should anything happen to either of us, I need you to know, right now, that I love you. And I didn't realize it until just now, but I've loved you for a long time."

She smiled but stayed silent.

Kalum swallowed. An awkward silence filled the room. It was deafening. "Is there anything that you wanted to say to me?" Kalum asked, clearing his throat nervously.

Her eyes widened. "Yes. You have to talk to Hack."

His head dropped. "I don't want to talk to Hack. I don't even want to look at Hack."

"Kalum, he's miserable. He blames himself for all of this. He says he's leaving."

Kalum looked up, a flash of anger coursing through him. "Maybe he should blame himself," he said, but he knew it wasn't true.

"Kalum, please. He didn't mean for this to happen. Talk to him."

He nodded. "Okay, where is he?"

"Get dressed," she said. "He's out there with his friend. I'll be in the next room. I have to talk to Katriana."

"What about?"

She looked back at him. "If she's going to join us in fighting a Dragon, then she needs to know our strategy."

As he got up, Trinn spoke again. "And Kalum," she said. "Blemm was right… about everything."

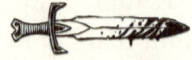

A smile spread across Kalum's face.

Kalum had to do a double-take as he exited the bedroom. Two identical Hacks sat in chairs facing each other beside the computer desk. They were dressed in matching clothes, and one of them, the one that looked devastated and miserable, was adjusting the collar on the shirt of the other. They both looked up as Kalum entered.

"I know what you're going to say," the miserable Hack said. "Just give me a few minutes and I'll be out of your hair forever."

"I don't want that," Kalum responded.

The man dropped his hands to his lap and took in a deep breath. "I can't do this anymore. I'm through." He pointed to his twin in front of him. "I'm leaving Mister Hax here to help you in whatever you need. He's very capable. I've made a few modifications. Just don't ask him about the weather."

"We need you, Hack."

He shook his head. "You don't need me. I'll just end up getting somebody else killed."

The reminder of Blemm's death stirred the grief that toiled in Kalum's gut. He sat heavily on the sofa and exhaled the breath he didn't know he'd been holding. "Why couldn't you have just waited a couple of days like I asked?"

Hack's face remained rigid, his jaw clenched. "I thought I could do it. I thought…"

"I told you not to."

"I know what you told me. But if it had worked, you'd be telling me what a genius I am."

"But it didn't work," Kalum yelled. "Did it? And now…"

Hack shut his eyes. "I know. I thought I could do it. I thought it would create a distraction. I didn't mean…"

Kalum sat up. "We didn't need a distraction. We need Blemm."

Hack stood. "I screwed up, okay? Do you think I don't know that?" He bent and picked up a blue bag that lay by his feet beside a rucksack and tossed it on the table. "I'm leaving that for you. Do what you want with it." The blue bag was clearly the loot that Hack had gained from his little adventure. It was pathetically small.

"Is that what you stole?" he mocked a laugh. "That little bag? Gods, I hope it was worth it. I hope Blemm's…" He couldn't finish the sentence. It was too cruel.

Hack stared back at him in silence, his eyes shining with tears. He picked up the rucksack and slung it over one shoulder. "I'm sorry," he said. Glancing once more at Mister Hax, he shook his head and walked out.

THIRTY TWO

CHAOS COMPOUNDED

KALUM SAT STILL on the sofa. How had everything gone so horribly wrong? The room was virtually silent. Only the quiet hum emanating from the biomech Mister Hax marred the quiet.

"You're not just going to let him go, are you?" Trinn stood in the bedroom doorway.

"It's his choice."

"Kalum, we need him."

Kalum shook his head. "He's done everything he was supposed to. There's nothing more—"

"Kalum." She looked at him, a sad expression on her face. "He needs us."

He shut his eyes. She was right, of course. She was always right. Hack was every bit as much a part of their group as anyone. He'd arguably done more than his fair share of the work. Kalum knew he hadn't meant for things to go so badly. It was a mistake.

He stood with an effort; his muscles ached. He did need Hack, he realized, for more than just his computer genius. He needed him for his friendship, his companionship, and support. He'd lost Blemm, there was no way back from that. He couldn't lose Hack as well.

"I'll see if I can catch him," he said and made his way toward the door.

"No need to rush," Mister Hax said. "I've tracked his datalink. He's just outside the door."

When Kalum opened the door, sure enough, there stood Hack, a look of concern on his face. Beside him stood a pudgy little man holding a weighty-looking suitcase.

"We've got big problems," Hack said and slipped past Kalum back into the room.

"I bumped into this man in the hall," Hack explained. He gestured to the other person. "His name is Puxley. He came looking for us."

"Looking for us?" Trinn said.

Puxley nodded. "I'm sorry. I tracked your friend Blemm to this floor." He looked around the room. "I'd hoped he'd be here."

"Who are you, exactly?" Kalum asked, concerned that someone would be tracking any of them.

"Until recently, I was in charge of the Biomech Command Center. But that's not important."

"Wait." Kalum held up a hand. "That is important. That's very important. You work for Borlan."

"I did," Puxley nodded. "Technically, I work for the Rhast, but I was on assignment to Borlan."

"The Rhast?" Kalum rubbed a hand through his hair, trying to understand. "How can you work for the Rhast?"

"Well, I am a Rhast."

Kalum blinked. He'd never actually met one of them before, but this man was surely not what he'd imagined a Rhast to look like.

"Kalum. Puxley is the one who installed the so-called modifications to the goblins, the mods that killed Blemm."

"Killed Blemm!" Puxley's face drained of color. "Oh, I'm so sorry." He squirmed uncomfortably. "The mods were created under Borlan's direct order, of course. I tried to warn him."

"Warn him?" Kalum said.

"Yes. You see, the goblins now have the capability to overload their own gammatronic logic circuits, their brains, if you will. This overload generates feedback to the reactor that ultimately results in a meltdown and an explosion. In other words, they self-destruct."

"That's what's been happening when their eyes turn green," Hack remarked. "But the overload probably takes a few seconds, which gave you time to destroy them before… boom."

"That's right," Puxley said. "The problem is that this is not an ordinary explosion. It's radioactive."

"What does that mean?" Kalum asked, ever confused.

"It creates radiation."

"Think of it like poison," Hack explained. "It poisons the air. A single goblin self-destructing creates a nominal amount of radiation. It's not good but still manageable."

"So, what are you telling me here?" Kalum said. "We were poisoned when that goblin exploded?"

"No," Hack said. "Well, actually… yes we were. But that's not the issue."

"The Rhast have recalled Borlan's goblins," Puxley said. "All of them outside of Central City. They're all moving to the coast, right now, to be picked up by Rhast boats."

"That's good news," Kalum said.

"Yes, but Borlan forced me to upload a new order to the biomechs. Once they all board the ships, they will all detonate simultaneously."

"Wow." Kalum sat back, trying to comprehend this news. He knew Borlan was a weasel, but this kind of back-stabbing treachery was a new low. "Can you recall them somehow?"

Puxley shook his head. "Even if I wasn't completely locked out of the Command Center, there's little chance I could stop the order. You see, I tied the detonation order to the command to board the ships, and the biomechs are already carrying out the program. The command is in progress."

Kalum shook his head, not really comprehending any of what Puxley was saying. "Can we contact the Rhast? Warn them?"

"No. My private Comm access to Rhast High Command was rescinded when Borlan locked me out."

"The only way to stop them is to destroy them," Hack said.

"Okay," Kalum nodded. "How many are we talking about?"

"Forty-two hundred."

Kalum choked. "Forty-two hundred! That would take every disruption grenade in the kingdom."

"No," Puxley said, unsnapping the latches on his suitcase. "That would take one Goblin Crusher Mega-Disruption Device." He opened the suitcase. "Like this one." Inside the case was a plain-looking black box. It was wrapped with various colored wires and cables and had two blinking green lights and a large black switch.

"What is that thing?" Kalum asked.

"I told you, it's a GCMD Device. I built it myself, in case of an emergency. It will take out every goblin within a quarter-mile radius. Just flip the switch and in ten seconds, zappo."

"Gods," Hack said, eyes ogling.

"Hold on. Is all this really necessary?" Kalum asked. "I mean, you said the goblins are set to destroy themselves anyway. I understand that means the loss of a couple of Rhast ships, but—"

"You don't understand, Kalum," Hack interrupted. "When forty-two hundred goblins explode at the same time, it will create a cloud of radiation so large that, depending on which way the wind blows, could wipe out every living thing in the kingdom."

"Are you serious?"

"He's absolutely right," Puxley said. "That's why it's so important that we stop them. I tried to explain this to Borlan, but he wouldn't listen. He's gone a bit crazy." He turned to Hack. "You have a very good understanding of all this. Are you sure you're not a Rhast?"

Hack smiled. "I read a lot. But I'll take that as a compliment."

"But you have this device," Kalum said. "Why are you here talking to us? Go shut down some goblins."

"I would, but we're talking about more than four thousand goblins congregating on a single beach in Sea View. The device must be placed in the middle of them in order to reach them all. I can't do that alone. I need your help."

"How long do we have?" Kalum asked, not needing a moment to consider.

"The Rhast ships should reach shore at around sunset tonight."

"It will take a while to drive to Sea View," Kalum figured. "We'd better get going."

"What about Mariah?" Hack asked.

"This is too important. She'll have to hold on a little while longer."

"Hack," Trinn said. "Where did you get this bag?" She was standing beside the computer station, looking at the blue bag on the table.

"I bought it," Hack said. "Do you recognize it?"

Trinn nodded. "It's a Bag of Holding, isn't it?"

"That's right. I saw it in a shop here in the city. I recognized it immediately. It's been years since I last saw it."

Hack remembered back to his first mission with the Thieves Guild. "Break into this particular house and steal the priceless artifact," they'd told him.

"What is this artifact?" he'd asked.

"A bag," was all they'd told him. He had assumed that the bag contained some kind of ancient relic or a fabulous jewel. He never suspected that the priceless artifact they referred to was the bag itself.

"What's a Bag of Holding?" Kalum asked.

"It's magic," Trinn answered. "The most powerful kind of magic—ancient magic. Its volume is unlimited, and no matter how much it carries, it always weighs and looks the same." She picked up the bag in one hand. "Like this."

"Unlimited?" Kalum asked.

Trinn nodded, her eyes still fixed on the bag. "They're incredibly rare. Just a handful of them are left in existence, from what I understand." She looked at Hack. "How much *did* you steal from that vault?"

THIRTY THREE

RESCUE RESCINDED

W HAT THE HELL do you mean, 'It's empty'?" Borlan stormed, red-faced, into the thirteenth floor vault. The word 'LORR' was painted on the back wall. It had been a long time since he'd seen the painted word, as it was usually covered by a massive stack of treasure. "There were two tons of gold in here."

"Thirty-nine hundred and twenty-six pounds, to be exact," Freedling corrected.

Borlan turned and pointed at the goblin that waited just outside the vault door. "You tell me!" he yelled. "How did two people, one of them barely the size of a winter goose, walk away with two tons of my gold?"

"Thirty-nine hundred and—"

"Freedling, SHUT UP!"

<*I have no logical explanation,*> the goblin stated.

"You're fired!" The king stamped his foot. "Do you hear me?" He jumped up and down, his face crimson red. "You're all fired!"

Mariah paced nervously around the penthouse suite. She'd gone over and over in her mind how the morning would play out. Folded in a scrap of parchment in her pocket, she carried eight of the "sleepy pills" that she had meticulously ground into a powder. Once she'd verified that GOB-82 was still obeying her commands, she'd slip the powder into Borlan's food or drink. It shouldn't take longer than a few minutes for the pills to take effect and for Borlan to go into a deep sleep.

The problem was that Borlan had not arrived. He was rarely late and never a no-show, so she wasn't overly nervous, but she'd prepared herself too long for him to skip today of all days.

At last, there came a knock and the door opened. In marched the chef's hat-wearing goblin, pushing the immaculate trolley that carried breakfast. But no Borlan.

<I'm sorry, Miss Mariah, but the king will likely not be joining you for breakfast this morning,> the goblin stated.

"What?" she said, tears threatening to form. She'd been ready! "Where is he?"

<He has other important matters to attend to, but he insisted I serve you just the same. He promised to make every effort to join you but suggested you start without him.>

Terrific, Mariah thought. Leave it to Borlan to screw up a good plan. But then… why not carry on with the plan? Not having to drug the king only made things that much simpler.

"GOB-82," she said. "Hand me that goblet." She pointed to the silver cup on the cart. The goblin promptly handed over the goblet. Perfect. It seemed to still be taking orders from her. Better to be sure, though. "GOB-82. Pat the top of your head and rub your tummy."

Without hesitation, the goblin performed the tasks, and with excellent dexterity she noted.

"GOB-82. Did the king give you any specific instructions before coming here this morning?" She needed to make sure Borlan hadn't told the goblin to strangle her or something if she attempted what she planned to attempt.

<Yes, ma'am. He did.>

Mariah rolled her eyes. "And what were those instructions?"

<I am to show you every courtesy, apologize for the king's tardiness, and under no circumstances am I to let you walk through

that door.> He gestured to the front door.

Well that figured. Borlan wasn't as trusting as he portrayed himself. Well, perhaps she could beat him at his own game.

"GOB-82, were those the king's exact words? 'Don't let her walk through that door'?"

<*Yes, ma'am. I can play back a recording of the order if you'd like.*>

"That won't be necessary. GOB-82, please empty a space beneath the trolley." She lifted the tablecloth that hung down on both sides of the cart.

<*Yes, ma'am,*> the goblin stated and began pulling the extra dishes and serving towels from the storage space beneath. While the goblin worked, Mariah gathered the breakfast plates and moved to the table to eat. Things were going perfectly. The meal was delicious as always.

Finally, it was time for the last step. When she'd finished eating, she let the goblin clear her dishes, leaving the king's meal uneaten on the table. Then, before it made to leave, she stopped it. "GOB-82," she said. "I want to play a game."

<*Yes, ma'am.*>

"It's a pretend game. We both will pretend that I am the extra dishes. I'll be stored in the trolley just like normal. And you will return the cart to where you normally take it."

The goblin's yellow eyes began to blink and it repeated, <*A pretend game.*>

"Yes, a pretend game. It's very fun. Let's play," she insisted. "By the way, where exactly do you take the trolley when you're finished here each morning?"

<*The service cart is taken to the Service Cart Storage Room on the basement level, adjacent to the kitchen.*>

"Perfect," Mariah said. "Now, you must follow the rules. You must act exactly the way you would normally act. As if I really am the extra dishes."

Yellow eyes blinked again.

"You won't be breaking any rules. This way, I'll never walk

out the door. You'll be pushing me, right?"

<That's correct, ma'am.>

"Splendid." Mariah bent down and climbed into the trolley, pulling her knees tightly to her chest in order to fit. When she was safely inside, she pulled the tablecloth down to hide herself.

"Okay," she called. "Let's play."

<Yes, ma'am.>

Borlan stomped along the corridor, Freedling in tow. His anger had reached a boiling point and he raved as he walked. "I want them found! I want them boiled alive!" He navigated through another unfortunate slaughter of goblins and continued his tirade. "Look at these losers! I don't have one competent minion in this entire stinking kingdom." They passed a trio of goblins that were working to move the body of the criminal that had been slain. "I take that back," he said, pointing to the body. "At least one of them was able to do something right. Find them, Freedling. I want them flayed in the streets. I want to hear their cries for mercy as their skin is peeled from their bodies!" He stopped and palmed the scanner for the secret elevator.

"What should we do with the body, Your Majesty?" Freedling asked, looking back at the dead man.

"Return him to his family, Freedling. We aren't savages."

The elevator door slid open and the king got inside.

"Your Majesty, where are you going?" Freedling asked, exasperated.

Borlan turned and jammed a finger against a button. As the door slid closed again, he looked at Freedling. "I'm going to breakfast."

While the others gathered their things, Hack made sure to clean the computer of any history or files that might reveal what they'd been up to. They planned to return to the tower for Mariah, but better to be safe than sorry. A small window at the bottom of the screen displayed the image from the bird that remained perched on the balcony rail of the penthouse. He gave it a cursory glance and froze. Enlarging the image to full-screen, he watched the display in awe.

"Kalum! Trinn!" he yelled. "Get in here."

The others, including Katriana and Puxley, rushed into the room. "What's the matter?" Kalum said, looking around for trouble.

"You are not going to believe this." Hack moved the cursor on the display and backed up the video a couple of minutes. They all crowded around and watched as Mariah, after all their time and effort and preparations for a rescue, escaped from the penthouse all on her own.

"I don't believe it," Kalum muttered.

"That is brilliant!" Trinn shouted.

"That's my girl," Katriana squealed in delight.

"Where is it taking her?" Kalum asked.

"Already on it," Puxley said, punching at his datapad. "It looks like the elevator is heading for the basement level."

"Time to go," Kalum shouted. "Grab your stuff."

Hack turned to his biomech. "This is a suicide mission, so I think this is probably the last time we'll see each other. I just want you to know… you're a handsome devil."

"As are you," Mister Hax replied.

The king exited the lift on the penthouse landing and nearly walked into the serving cart being pushed by the goblin. "Is my breakfast ready for me?" he asked.

The goblin's yellow eyes began blinking rapidly.

"Well? Do I have breakfast waiting for me inside?"

<*Yes, sir. Your breakfast is inside.*>

"Good." He strode past the cart and triggered the palm scanner to open the door, ignoring the golden armored man who stood on guard.

The suite was suspiciously quiet as he entered. Borlan stood in the entry and called out, "Mariah? I'm sorry I'm late. It's been a very trying morning. I've so much to tell you."

There was no reply.

"Mariah, my dear," he called again and began to rush through the suite looking. His breakfast was sitting neatly on the table, but there was no setting for Mariah. He searched all about. Not on the balcony, not in the sitting room. Not in the bedroom. Not in the bathroom. His heart began to race as the reality of the situation began to dawn on him. When he spotted the stack of dishes and towels on the floor, his eyes widened in realization.

The king raced back out onto the elevator landing. "She's gone," he said to the armored man. "The goblin. She must have been in the cart."

The armored man ran into the suite, then seconds later returned. "I'll go find her," he said and rushed to the elevator.

Borlan's blood pounded in his ears. "You better!" he yelled behind him.

THIRTY FOUR

DRAGON DISCOVERED

THE CART HAD stopped moving and Mariah heard a door open and shut. She was in complete darkness. She waited several minutes and, hearing no further sounds, she rolled herself out from underneath the serving trolley. Standing slowly, she felt about with her hands to locate the door.

Opening the door, she peeked out into an empty corridor. There seemed no sign of anyone up or down the hall, and she spotted the elevator in one direction. Dashing from the storage room, she raced up the hall and ducked into a deserted enclave just as a pair of goblins turned a corner ahead of her and came walking up the corridor.

She held her breath and pressed herself against the wall as the goblins passed by her. Looking up, she saw a camera near the ceiling pointed directly at her. Once the goblins were out of sight, she took a deep breath and continued toward the elevator.

Hack stood crammed in the elevator with the others, his fingers racing over his datapad.

"Aha! I got her. She's on the basement level, darting around like a frenzied squirrel."

"Security has been alerted to her escape," Puxley said, his own datapad in hand. "They'll be looking for her."

"Looks like she's trying to make it to the lift," Hack remarked.

"She'll probably want to get to the lobby," Kalum said. "Let's get out there."

Mariah made a final sprint to the elevator and slammed her hand on the call button. She nervously bounced on the balls of her feet, waiting for the door to open. The seconds passed like hours.

<*Wait,*> came a mechanical voice, and she tensed in near-panic.

The goblin came beside her and took her arm. <*Mariah Rothburn, are you still pretending to be extra dishes?*>

Mariah inhaled an excited breath of air. "GOB-82, I'm so glad to see you!"

<*Are we still playing your game?*>

"Yes we are," Mariah said as the elevator door opened. "Come with me."

Kalum stepped into the lobby, the others crowded behind him. He dropped his satchel of belongings onto the floor and surveyed the area. Scores of gamblers were making their way to the game room for the start of the tournament, but there was no sign of Mariah. "Where is she?" he said.

Hack turned and pointed to the next elevator over to the right. "She's coming out now."

The door to the lift opened with a chime and out stepped Mariah, being led by a goblin, her arm tightly in its grip.

Kalum dropped any pretense of remaining unnoticed and pulled GOBSlayer from beneath his cloak.

"No, Kalum," Mariah yelled, looking up at the last second. "It's okay. It's with me."

<*Physical altercations will not be tolerated.*> the goblin said. <*This is your only warning.*>

"Mariah," Kalum said, looking at her. She looked the same as he remembered. But there was something changed. She was older of course, but also there was a confidence about her he'd never seen.

The girl, the daughter of the baron, so aloof and gentle, was gone, replaced by a poised and coolheaded woman, who'd engineered her own escape by commandeering her own goblin.

"We have to go," Hack interrupted his thoughts.

The wall above the elevators suddenly burst into flames. They all ducked low, Puxley diving into the open elevator. Kalum spotted a man in gold armor standing not twenty feet away, another fireball forming in his hands. This had to be their Gold Dragon. He didn't look so tough, but Kalum knew enough about Dragons to not be fooled by his appearance.

The goblin that had accompanied Mariah suddenly surged forward, pushing Mariah to the ground as the Dragon's next fireball hit it full in the body. It burst into flames and slumped lifeless to the floor. Mariah screamed out and rolled safely away.

"Get behind me," Trinn shouted, and with a word from her lips, a shimmering shield formed in front of them, deflecting another fireball that the man in gold had launched. "Remember what to do," she added.

Trinn's shield was brutally tested as the Dragon hurled not only fireballs but also jets of ice shards that shattered against the barrier. Next was a stream of flames that washed around them, the heat singing the hair on Kalum's neck. The attacks were powerful, and finally, the Dragon paused, showing a moment of fatigue.

"Now," Trinn shouted. And as she'd instructed them all, they rushed behind her in a tight group and then darted away from each other, spreading out in a line as Trinn called another spell. There was a blur of light as Kalum took a position to Trinn's left, GOBSlayer ready. Glancing sideways, he saw that there were now a line of a dozen people facing the Dragon. Trinn's illusion made it appear that there were three Hacks, three Katrianas, and even two copies of himself, each wielding a copy of GOBSlayer. Even Trinn herself had tripled in number. Mariah, who had no weapon, wisely stayed back, ducking defensively against the wall.

Kalum knew these illusionary others were of no use in the fight, but served only to confuse their opponent. It had the desired effect, Kalum thought, for he himself had no idea which of the others were the real ones.

But the Dragon apparently thought he knew the real from the fake, and he fired off another fireball at one of the Trinns. The sparkling barrier deflected the attack, but the impact caused the shield to flicker and warble. Trinn's magic was being stretched dangerously thin.

Kalum watched the Gold Dragon closely, waiting for a sign that he was weakening. A narrow bead of sweat dripped down the man's forehead, and his breathing was fast, but his attacks were unrelenting. More flame and more ice-shards battered at Trinn's shield, and in one catastrophic moment, a ball of fire penetrated the barrier and engulfed one of the Hacks. Trinn shouted out and the flames died away quickly, but the damage had been done. Hack lay curled in a blackened heap on the ground. Trinn shouted in anger and the shield brightened with restored vigor. The dragon, heartened by his successful attack, increased his barrage. The impacts against the shield were deafening, but Kalum kept his concentration. Waiting, waiting. Finally, the attacks paused and the Dragon slumped ever so slightly in exhaustion.

"I'm going," Kalum shouted to Trinn through clenched teeth. And heart racing, he charged through the shield, driving toward the dragon with reckless anger. He only barely noticed that two other Kalums were charging alongside him. The Dragon took a chance and launched a fireball, but it rocketed directly through its target.

Kalum drew close to the dragon and swung his sword across from the left. The Dragon, already off-guard trying to dodge an illusory sword that was thrown by an illusory Kalum, shot out a hand, blasting an invisible force that punched Kalum from his feet, but not before he was struck in the ribs by

GOBSlayer's blade. The Dragon cried out in pain. Kalum was thrown backward, leaving his breath behind, and landed hard on the tiled floor, sliding to a stop.

He sat up, still struggling for breath, and witnessed the strangest sight he could imagine. Half a dozen people—three Katrianas, two Hacks, and a Trinn—charged at the Dragon, who had dropped to his knees, clutching his side. They jumped on him and landed several blows before being tossed aside.

Trinn's illusion broke and all of their magical duplicates dispersed into thin air. Kalum saw with relief that the Hack who'd been scorched by the fireball had actually been one of the phantoms. Trinn had expertly manipulated the illusion to show Hack being burned, presumably to fool the Dragon.

Mariah ran to Kalum's side. "Are you okay?" she gasped. Kalum nodded and accepted her help getting to his feet.

Trinn stalked forward, a smoking and sparking ball of fire hovering at her shoulder, and stood before the battered Dragon. He looked back at her, both fear and defiance in his eyes. "Finish it," he said.

The fireball she'd conjured vanished. "No." She shook her head wearily. "This isn't the way…"

She said more, but her words were drowned by the uproar of commotion that came from the far side of the lobby. The Dragon laughed and spoke a final word, and then he too dispersed into smoke and was gone.

Kalum turned toward the sound. With a thunder of heavy footsteps, an army of goblins, each one carrying a sword, marched in their direction. He gripped GOBSlayer tightly, but he knew it was helpless. Hotel guests and gamblers crowded along the edges of the lobby, watching the confusion in disbelief.

The others—Trinn, Hack, Katriana, and even Puxley, dragging his suitcase beside him—came to stand with Kalum as goblins spread out to surround them. Trinn struggled just to remain standing.

"What do you think? Give up? Or go out fighting?"

THIRTY FIVE

AN APPREHENSIVE
APPROACH

LUCKILY, KALUM DIDN'T have to answer Hack's question. A scream rose up from one of the hotel guests. At the front doors, a screeching, almost maniacal yell echoed through the cavernous lobby. "We back!"

The doors crashed open as a virtual flood of green creatures stormed inside. Goblins! Real, honest to Gods goblins. They carried swords, spears, sticks, and rocks. Kalum even saw one wielding a large drumstick of meat. They screamed and shouted profanities as they swarmed the biomechs. Spitting and laughing, they overwhelmed their mechanical look-alikes. Kalum grinned. Blemm's distraction had arrived. Even in death, his old friend had come through to save his neck one last time. One of the creatures, a fat, slower-moving goblin with a sword, came to Kalum. "Honor I am, greet GolaStap," he garbled.

Kalum bowed his head slightly. "Thank you for coming."

The fat goblin grinned widely and belched, spreading his arms wide. "Blemm make happen." He looked around. "Blemm?"

Kalum shook his head. "Blemm was killed fighting the biomechs."

The goblin's face scrunched in anger. "Sad I am. Great man Blemm." And with a nod, he turned and shouted into the chaos of the battle. "For Blemm. And for Glach!" He charged headlong into the maw, sword flailing.

"We should really get out of here while we can," Hack suggested.

Kalum nodded. "Let's go."

After squeezing their way past the continuous inflow of goblins, they stepped out to the curb. "Flag a car, would you?" Kalum said to Hack.

Mariah turned to him with a smile. "Thank you, Kalum, for coming to my rescue. You're a wonderful man." She hugged him tightly, saying, "You've always been my knight in shining armor." A car pulled up behind her and Kalum leaned over and opened the rear door. To the driver he shouted, "Baron Rothburn will pay you triple your regular rate to take this woman home to Lenshire."

The driver grinned. "You got it, Mac."

"Kalum," Mariah pulled away. "I'm going with you."

Kalum shook his head and began to protest, but Katriana was suddenly there beside them. "Oh, the hell you are," she said, her tone leaving no question. "You're taking yourself home to your father. He's worried himself half-crazy about you."

Mariah sat reluctantly in the car. "When will we see each other again?" she asked.

Kalum smiled. "Someday soon, I promise."

"Be careful, okay?" she said.

Kalum shut the door.

Katriana looked up at him, her eyes rolling. "Kalum, I'm going with you," she mocked Mariah's words. "Please."

They funneled their way through the parking lot, and Hack invited Puxley to ride with him on the cycle. Puxley agreed with a grin, seemingly excited by the offer. He passed off the suitcase to Kalum. "Meet you in Sea View," Kalum told them.

When the rest of them reached his car, Kalum wasn't entirely surprised to find Elbore sitting sidelong in the open backseat. Somehow he knew their paths would cross again.

"You wouldn't be travelling to Sea View would you?" Elbore said, sitting up.

"As a matter of fact," Kalum replied, smiling, "that's exactly where we're headed.

Elbore nodded. "I had a feeling. I thought I might be able to find a ride to Rhastor there. I understand there are some ships arriving soon."

"You don't know the half of it," Kalum told him. He loaded the suitcase into the trunk, and then they all climbed into the car, Trinn in front with Kalum, and Katriana with Elbore in back.

The drive to Sea View was quiet with only sparse conversation. Kalum explained to Elbore, as best he could remember, about the danger the goblins posed.

"I knew, of course, about the double-cross that Borlan devised," Elbore explained. "But I had no idea of the aftermath. Borlan's lost his mind."

Some time later, Trinn turned and said to the old man, "I'm glad you've decided to go look for your family in Rhastor."

"I haven't high hopes," Elbore told her. "The chances are slim of finding them alive, but I have to try."

"Well, I wish you the best of luck."

Katriana was uncharacteristically quiet. Kalum feared the encounter with the Dragon had shaken the nobby. He hoped she had regained her wits when they reached Sea View.

The reality of what they were heading toward had not fully taken hold in Kalum's mind: more than four thousand goblins. What a sight that would be. But a growing sense of dread threatened to overwhelm him with every mile.

He knew what detonating a gamma-disruption bomb would do to him. He tried to think of another option, but there was no choice. He alone was their best chance of reaching the center of the crowd of goblins. Leaving the task to any of the others not only risked that person's life, but conceivably the lives of the entire kingdom. He gripped the steering wheel tightly, his nervousness rising. What would it feel like? He'd never feared death before, but then, death had never been so clearly scheduled for him. Even in his darkest times, when the odds were heavily stacked against him, there had always been a chance, a glimmer of hope for survival. Now though…

He thought of Blemm. The loss of the warrior weighed on all of his friends, he knew, but Kalum felt a particular stab of sorrow now as he drove. He imagined the brute sitting behind him, wind in his hair, encouraging them all with talk of honor, duty, and the thrill of what was to come. He was fearless, and Kalum needed his courage now more than ever. Blemm's optimism had always been more than enough to dilute Kalum's fears. Without it, there was only helplessness.

Mariah was fuming. How dare he stick her in a taxi after everything she'd been through? She was not some little child to be shuffled away when things got dangerous. After all, she'd escaped the tower all on her own.

She exhaled a tightly-held breath and let herself relax, closing her eyes. On the other hand, Kalum was probably just concerned for her safety. He was a good man. He'd risked everything to come to her aid, and she did appreciate his thoughtfulness in sending her home while everyone else rushed into danger.

Her eyes popped open. "Oh, to hell with that," she said, leaning forward. "Driver! How would you like to triple your fare?"

THIRTY SIX

BORLAN'S BROODING

BACK IN LORR Tower, King Borlan brooded and pouted in his penthouse suite. How lonely it felt without Mariah to talk to. Everything was going wrong. Everyone was against him. He'd lost his gold, his goblins, his magician, and now he'd lost Mariah. It was all Rothburn's fault, and Elbore's. And it was the Rhast's fault and their pathetic goblins. He was on the verge of considering his own blame in the matter when the door opened and in walked Freedling.

"What do *you* want?" Borlan said.

"I'm sorry to interrupt you while you're... moping, Your Majesty, but I have news."

"What is it?"

"Rhast ships have been spotted near the coast, sir. They should reach land within the hour."

Borlan nodded. "Good. Let's see how they like their goblins when they explode."

"Yes, about that, sir," Freedling looked at him over his glasses. "Have you considered how the Rhast will react when they learn you've destroyed their ships?"

"How they'll react?"

Freedling cleared his throat. "Yes, Your Majesty. I doubt they'll take the news calmly."

"No," Borlan grinned. "They'll be furious. They'll think twice before pushing around King Borlan again, I'll tell you that."

"Have you also considered the fact that with the goblins

destroyed, the kingdom has no army? No defenses whatsoever, in fact. Should the Rhast decide to, as you say, push you around, how will you stop them?"

Borlan blinked rapidly. He had not considered that possibility... at all. It had never occurred to him that anyone would challenge his authority. No one ever had.

"We've got to raise an army!" Borlan stammered, jumping to his feet. "I must return to the palace and see to it immediately. Freedling, don't just stand there. Arrange for a car!"

"Yes, Your Majesty." Freedling bowed his head and left.

They arrived late in the afternoon as the sun was dipping low on the horizon. It took them a while to finally get to the beach, as the sleepy town of Sea View had been invaded by thousands of onlookers from around the kingdom come to see the goblins' final destination. Kalum sent a message to Hack, letting him know they'd arrived and then retrieved the suitcase from the trunk. As they came to the low fence at the top of the beach, Trinn let out a gasp of amazement. The wide beach was a muddle of green. Goblins stood shoulder to shoulder in a horde so large, she couldn't begin to estimate their numbers.

The crowd that had gathered along the fence held an almost festive atmosphere. People laughed and hollered taunts at the goblins. Some held up hand-written signs that read, GO HOME, GOBLINS, and DON'T HURRY BACK, and other messages of affection.

Three metal ships, troop carriers, rested on the shoreline, heavy wheels along the bottom of their hulls having driven them up to the beach. The flat metal front of each ship was lowered to the beach like wide gangplanks. Men bustled around the ships, preparing to load them with goblins.

Kalum pointed toward the horizon, where the shapes of three additional ships could be seen far out on the ocean. "There are more ships coming." He set the suitcase on the ground and opened the latches.

"Do you think they'll try to stop you?" Katriana asked.

"The goblins? I don't know," Kalum said, lifting out the black box. "Probably not if they're programmed to just board the ships. But who knows for sure?" He turned to them. "Keep an eye on me. If for some reason I can't make it to the center, or if something happens to me, you have to finish the job. We can't let them board those boats."

He turned and threw a leg over the railing and half-hopped, half-slid down the embankment to the beach. The box was small enough that he could carry it under one arm, which was fortunate in case he needed to use GOBSlayer.

"Hey," someone from the crowd called. "You crazy? Those are still goblins."

Kalum ignored the warning and made his way slowly toward the horde. When he reached them, he took a deep breath and pushed his way through. As he maneuvered farther and farther, he called out to the goblins, hoping to be dismissed as one of the Rhast sailors, "Don't crowd," he shouted. "Be as orderly as possible and prepare to board."

The goblins moved aside slowly as he touched them on the shoulders. Squeezing between them was difficult with the added bulk of the box, but step by step, he was getting there.

"Quite a sight, huh?" Hack stepped up beside Trinn. "An ugly sight, but a sight."

"Hack." Trinn smiled. "Glad you're still with us."

Hack nodded. "I am too. Where's Kalum?"

Trinn pointed to the mass of goblins. "In there."

"What!" Hack shouted, squinting to try and find him in the maw of green. "What the hell is he doing?"

"He's doing what we came here to do," Trinn said, confused

by his reaction.

"But he can't... It'll..." He looked genuinely worried.

"What's wrong with you, Hack? There was no question that it would be Kalum who took the device."

"Trinn, it can't be Kalum. We've got to stop him."

"Hack." She grabbed him by the arm and spun him around to face her. "Tell me what is going on. Now."

THIRTY SEVEN

GOBLINS GALORE

KALUM STOPPED AND looked over the heads of the goblins, a sea of green all around him. It was hard to judge, but it looked like he was near the center. Perhaps a hundred feet or so more to go toward the ocean and he'd be ready. The realization of what he was doing still tingled at the back of his mind, but all of his attention now was on knocking out these goblins before they could unleash their damage.

<Kalum Tinbrook,> said one of the biomechs.

Kalum spun around to find a red-eyed goblin staring back at him.

<You are under arrest for crimes against the kingdom.>

"Not today," Kalum said and turned to keep moving. He'd only gotten a few feet before another goblin, its eyes red, turned on him.

<Come quietly,> it said. *<Physical altercations will not be tolerated.>*

Damn it. He was so close now. He looked around. In the vast field of green goblins, among a star field of yellow eyes, flecks of red began to appear as the discovery of his presence disseminated among the goblins. Then he saw her. Far to the back of the horde, Trinn was pushing her way toward him.

Well, he wasn't about to wait for more goblins around him to realize who he was. He lowered his head and pushed on, all the way yelling out to them, "Prepare to board the transports. Face the ships and move in an orderly fashion."

Trinn pushed desperately into the goblins. She had to reach him before… Hack had revealed to her Kalum's secret. She knew that detonating the device would likely kill him. Fear raced through her, fear of losing him. But also anger. How could he be so stupid?

A red-eyed goblin turned around in front of her. *< Trinn Shadowmoon, >* it said.

Kalum pressed ahead, pushing and dodging through goblins. Four of them blocked his path and he was forced to act when their eyes had turned green. He pulled GOBSlayer and swung in a sweeping motion, slicing cleanly across the necks of three of them. The rapid pulse of the sword's disruptor vibrated in his grip. The fourth goblin swung overhand at him and he moved desperately to block the blow, but the blade of the goblin's sword deflected off of GOBSlayer's cross guard and hit Kalum's wrist. By some miracle, his datalink took the force of the strike, shattering in a wisp of smoke.

The goblin grabbed at his arm and pulled him toward it, causing Kalum to lose his grip on the black box, which fell to the ground beside him. Spinning out of its grasp, Kalum thrust GOBSlayer into its chest and the creature fell, eyes dark. But as he turned to retrieve the box, it was nowhere to be seen. He turned all about. Where had it gone?

Then, from the corner of his eye, he spotted a miniature person rushing away. It was Katriana of course, her arms wrapped wide around the box, which looked massive against her tiny frame. She dodged this way and that between more goblins, carrying the device toward its necessary location.

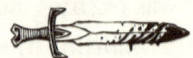

From the wayside, Puxley turned to Hack. "He needs to be underneath it."

Hack glanced at him, before turning back toward the beach. "What are you talking about?"

"I heard what you told Trinn about Kalum. The only safe

place is directly beneath it. Basically, the GCMD detonates outward and upward. If he can be under it, he might be safe."

Hack yanked his datapad from his side and rapidly tapped a message to Kalum.

"Damn," Hack shouted. "The message won't go through for some reason."

Kalum slashed and stabbed at the swarm of goblins closing in ever closer, paying attention to the ones with eyes of green. While his focus was on the fight, a small part of his brain waited fearfully for what was coming: the detonation of the disruptor bomb and what it would feel like. What would come after?

A woman's cry rose up, and Kalum looked to see Katriana being held above the head of a goblin and carried away. She no longer held the device. Had she activated it? He had to assume she hadn't, so he turned and fought his way in the direction he'd seen her run, hoping he could find it in the chaos.

Hack raced down the beach, yelling at the top of his lungs, but his voice sounded small over the commotion all around him. He had to warn Kalum before it was too late. He spotted Trinn in the crowd of goblins. She'd encompassed herself in a glowing shield of magic and was pushing through the beasts, launching bolts of magic to clear her path. Hack yelled out her name, but she either couldn't hear him or was not able to stop and respond.

He stopped and scanned the beach, searching desperately for Kalum. He even jumped into the air a couple of times, trying to get a better look over the tops of the goblins, but no luck.

Kalum twisted around a pair of red-eyed biomechs and thrust GOBSlayer backward, skewering one of them completely and thus piercing the other behind it. They both fell as he pulled his sword free. He turned to continue the fight and saw it. Sitting in the sand, like an abandoned toy, Puxley's device lay in front of him. Without stopping to ponder the consequences, he dove forward and slapped the black switch. The green lights on the box began flashing red.

Strangely, he just stared at the lights, lost in them, and the world seemed to go quiet around him. This was it. Everything he'd done in his life, everyone he'd known or met, every action he'd taken, had all led him to this. A high-pitch whistle from the box pierced the air and the noise seemed to wake Kalum from his daze. Beneath the whistle, he could again hear the roar of the ocean. He rolled to one side just in time to see a goblin's sword arch down into his shoulder. He yelled out from the stinging wound and stabbed GOBSlayer upward into his attacker. The ear-splitting whistle increased ten-fold, and then in an instant of chest-crushing pain, everything went black.

Trinn screamed as the goblins fell. They toppled over onto one another, lifeless puppets, their strings cut. But she knew that somewhere, Kalum was among them. Tears streamed down her face as she climbed on hands and knees over mechanical bodies, searching for him. She prayed in anguish as she crawled to any god who would hear her to be merciful to the man she loved, to be merciful to *her*.

THIRTY EIGHT

BIOMECH BLAST

KALUM OPENED HIS eyes with a start. He was sitting in a forest clearing surrounded by giant ever-reaching dark oak trees. The bark of the enormous trees appeared almost black. A small campfire crackled before him and he rubbed his eyes. Checking his shoulder, he saw the wound he'd just received from the goblin was gone.

He jerked at the sound of rustling brush and the distinctive cracking of footsteps in the distance. From the foliage, a large man stepped into the clearing, a slain deer slung over one mighty shoulder. Kalum blinked, not believing his own eyesight. It was Blemm.

"The hunting here is fantastic," Blemm said.

Kalum opened his mouth to reply, but he snapped it closed again, fearing that speaking would break whatever dream or hallucination this was. Or was this something else?

Blemm dropped the deer carcass on the ground beside the fire. "What a glorious place to camp, huh?" He lowered himself and sat across from Kalum. "Still, there's something ominous about this forest, almost as if it's watching us."

"Where are we?" Kalum dared to speak.

Blemm laughed, deep and beautiful. "Does it really matter?"

"No, I suppose not."

Blemm sighed and rested back on his elbows. "That was a very brave thing you did."

Kalum stared over the fire, not knowing what to say.

Blemm looked up at him. "On the beach, remember? There aren't many who would risk everything like that."

"You would have."

"Well, I *am* pretty brave," Blemm chuckled.

"I'm not," Kalum said. "I could have saved you, Blemm. But I was too afraid. I'm so sorry."

"Stop it! You're the bravest man I ever knew. You did what you had to do, and if you hadn't," he looked around at the forest encircling them, "well, for one, we wouldn't be together in this glorious place."

Kalum looked down into the fire. "We all knew what we were getting into," he said quietly, remembering the words Blemm had said to him.

Kalum looked up, the smoke from the fire was distorting his view of his friend. He tried to think of a better way to broach the subject, but then he just asked. "Are we dead?"

"You're not," Blemm said and the smoke thickened. "You're only dreaming, but we will meet again, someday."

"I hope so."

"You're a good man, Kalum Tinbrook," came Blemm's distant voice, but Kalum could no longer see him. "Trinn was right when she said that you're the heart of our group."

"…the heart," his voice echoed.

The smoke began to sting Kalum's eyes and he closed them tight. Suddenly, he lurched forward, his chest aching as his heart began to beat on its own for the first time in years.

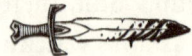

He opened his eyes. Trinn sat crouched over him, crying tears of joy at seeing him awaken. They held each other there for a long time before the others joined them. Hack patted him on the chest. "Told you," he said with a grin. "I never had a doubt."

Elbore stood stoically, looking around at the goblin-littered beach.

Katriana was giddy with excitement. "I've never been a part of a team before," she admitted. "Always told I was too small." She nodded. "Now I see why you do this stuff!"

Puxley picked up the half-crumpled black box and held it to his chest, repeating to himself, "It worked. It worked."

"I guess someone should go explain this to the Rhast," Hack said.

"Am I mistaken," Elbore said, still looking out across the beach, "or does this not seem like enough goblins."

They all looked around. "How can you tell?" Trinn asked. "They're everywhere."

"No, he's right," Hack added. "There aren't nearly four thousand."

"Oh gods," Puxley said, gazing out at the ocean. "Those ships." He pointed a shaking hand. "They aren't coming in. They're leaving. They're already loaded with goblins."

As though they'd been waiting to be discovered, the ships exploded in a flash of light. Plumes of green smoke rose up from the wreckage, blooming into dense clouds.

"Trinnity," Elbore shouted. "Shield the beach."

Trinn acted fast. She gathered all of her strength and summoned a gigantic barrier that she stretched wide and high across the shoreline. The shockwave hit just seconds later. The impact was enormous. Her knees buckled, and the shimmering shield wavered and flickered from the force.

Elbore stood beside her, his face scrunched up in concentration and his arms waving back and forth at his sides, as if pushing something away. Trinn felt the gentlest hint of a breeze at her back. He must be creating a wind, she thought, to push away the poisonous cloud created from the blast.

Trinn had never learned to manipulate the weather, as it was among the more difficult kinds of magic. Creating a wind was perhaps the hardest, moving something as insubstantial as the air. She watched Elbore work his power.

He was obviously struggling, having to push against the ocean breeze that was blowing onshore. Sweat began beading on his forehead, and still, the wind was pushing toward them, not away.

Trinn came behind him and gently laid her hands on his shoulders. She couldn't help him directly with the magic, but she could add her own strength to his. She felt a powerful rush as energy flooded from her body. Elbore was struggling more than she'd realized. She tightened the muscles in her legs and gripped tightly to his shoulders as a strong wind suddenly gusted from behind.

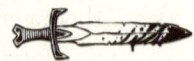

The green mushrooms hung in the air like toxic trees on the ocean. Kalum and the others stood together, perfectly still, perfectly silent, and stared. On the distant horizon, as though scattered by a giant hand, the blooming clouds dispersed outward over the Infinite Sea.

A cheer rose up as the crowd above the beach, having witnessed everything, erupted in excited applause. They shouted and waved in celebration.

But Kalum paid them little attention. Trinn and Elbore had both collapsed in the sand. He rushed to Trinn and held her head, repeating her name, and gently tried to wake her. Hack was assisting Elbore in a similar fashion when Mariah arrived, running across the beach.

"What's happened?" Mariah asked.

"I think they overdid themselves with magic," Kalum answered.

Mariah turned to Puxley and pointed up the beach. "There, those Pelantex shrubs. Bring me some, quickly." She looked at Katriana. "Kat, I need a wet cloth." Katriana raced away toward the water, tearing away a piece of her skirt that she wore.

"Can you help her?" Kalum asked as Mariah knelt beside Trinn. She shook her head. "I don't know."

Puxley returned first and handed Mariah a small leafy branch from the Pelantex. Mariah tore off a few of the leaves and began smashing them with her thumb against the palm of her other hand.

Kalum rocked nervously, running his hand over Trinn's head. Only moments had passed, but it felt like an eternity.

"Open her mouth for me," Mariah said.

Kalum reached over and pressed his fingers against her chin and slowly worked open her clenched jaw. Mariah bent forward and placed a wad of the mashed Pelantex leaves under Trinn's tongue, then closed her mouth again.

Taking the wet cloth from Katriana, she spread it across Trinn's forehead.

"Will she be okay?" Kalum asked.

"We'll know in a second," Mariah said.

"A second?"

Trinn's eyes popped open and darted all about. She turned to one side and spit out the leaves. "What happened?" she gagged. "Are we safe?"

Kalum wiped his eyes. "We're safe," he told her. "You and Elbore... Elbore!"

"He's okay," Hack said.

"Are you sure?" Trinn said, sitting up. Elbore lay still beside Hack, his eyes shut peacefully.

Hack nodded. "He was awake for a bit. He seemed happy to hear the crowd cheering. Then he closed his eyes and fell asleep."

Trinn slumped back onto the sand, tears running down to her ears. "We showed them, didn't we Elbore?" she said. "We showed them."

After some long moments of silence, Hack turned slowly to Kalum. "Someone should really go explain this to the Rhast."

"I'll tell you what. Borlan had better find a large rock to hide under after this," Katriana said. "The Rhast are going to hunt him down."

Hack shook his head and pulled out his datapad. "I don't think the Rhast will have to worry about Borlan for much longer."

The limousine raced up the highway. Borlan sat in the back with his legs up, typing out a message on his datapad. He informed his chamberlain at the castle to have things prepared for his return: a drawn bath, his favorite dinner, and his chief war strategist at the ready.

Without warning, the car swerved violently to the right, coming to a stop alongside the road.

Borlan triggered the button to lower the privacy screen between the back of the limo and the driver.

"What the hell are you doing up there?" he yelled. "Why have we stopped?"

The driver turned to face him, and Borlan gasped. It was Hack, one of the criminals from the tower. He recognized him immediately from pictures, but now he looked bizarre with a wide grin and glowing green eyes.

"Oh, crap," Borlan said, remembering his green-eyed goblins.

"How about this weather?" Mister Hax asked cheerfully, before his logic circuits overloaded and an explosion engulfed the car.

A hundred feet up the road, a little black bird sat perched on the branch of a bare and tired tree. It watched, unblinking, as the limousine burned.

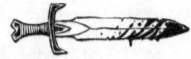

"Nope. King Borlan won't be a problem any longer." Hack snapped his datapad closed and tucked it back into his coat.

EPILOGUE

EVER AFTER

THE DAYS AND weeks following the incident at Sea View were a tumultuous time for Lorr. With the absence of the biomechs, and the death of the king, there came a smattering of uprisings, launched by those angered at the state of the kingdom and by those fearful of an uncertain future.

Oddly, it was those who had been most feared and most persecuted, the magic users, who arose as peacekeepers, quelling revolts where they ignited and urging order and stability. It took time, but at last, an uneasy calm fell over the land, a welcome respite from the unpleasantness of recent years.

Since Borlan had no siblings and had produced no heir, a multitude of ambitious people, the rich and the powerful, came out to voice their desire and sometimes, their perceived right to ascend the throne. And yet, when it was suggested that these prospects, many of whom had perpetrated and profited from barbaric spectacles like the Fire Trials, should themselves compete for the throne inside an arena in a battle-to-the-death style contest, most of them quickly withdrew their names from contention. In the end, however, the king was not chosen by Battle Royale, but instead, reasonable minds prevailed, and on a warm day in spring, Lorr held its first free election. The people of Lorr were for once allowed to choose their own leader.

Not surprising to many, Baron Rothburn of Lenshire was the clear choice. He was recognized as being fair and just, and his small part in the events leading to Borlan's death did not fare poorly among the common people of Lorr.

The baron's daughter, Mariah, who instantly became a princess and the future queen, opened a series of health clinics across the land, offering care to the entire kingdom. Her venture was a tremendous success, and she soon became the kingdom's new 'It-girl,' with dozens of wealthy young suiters competing for her attention and affection.

As King Rothburn's first act of business, a new deal was struck with the Rhast, and while the export of much-needed metal from the kingdom ceased, new technological gadgets and equipment were still made available in Lorr. In fact, to better distribute their goods throughout the land, the Rhast reached a secondary agreement with an unlikely partner, the goblins of lost glory, who have since built a chain of convenient one-stop-shopping technology stores called GobShops. To date, the stores are reputedly doing quite a business.

It was six months after Blemm's death, when Kalum, Trinn, and Hack gathered together on a small potato farm in the south of Lorr to honor and remember their dear friend. The farm was in some disrepair, the fields needing obvious tending and the little farmhouse wanted for paint. On a shady hillock, Blemm's mighty hammer stood planted in the grass, marking the spot where his remains had been laid.

Kalum stood beside Sophia, Blemm's widow, on that grassy grade and admired the old warrior's resting place. The head of his hammer, set permanently with mortar, had been beautifully engraved by a local ironworker with a single word: BLEMM. Its handle, long and sturdy, reached skyward, just slightly off-vertical.

"He loved you, you know," Sophia told Kalum.

Kalum looked at her, but he stayed silent. Her graying hair flittered in the warm breeze and her sun-bronzed face wrinkled with a peaceful smile. "He loved going off with you," she continued, "adventuring around the kingdom, or whatever you do." She reached up and put her hand on his shoulder. "He just loved it," her voice cracked and her eyes filled with tears.

"Sophia." Kalum turned to her and took her hand in his own. "I'm so sorry."

She shook her head. "No, it's all right," she said, quickly regaining her composure. "I'm fine. It's funny, just when I think I've grieved all I can, I remember some silly thing he used to do, or some silly thing he'd say, and it just all comes back."

"I know what you mean," Kalum said. "I miss him terribly."

Just then, Trinn and Hack came up behind them. Trinn slid her arm around Kalum's waist and gave him a gentle squeeze. Hack stood opposite Sophia and looked solemnly at Blemm's hammer. He'd not spoken more than three words since they'd arrived.

"Thank you so much for coming," Sophia said. "It means a lot." She lifted her head and sniffed, looking out across the fields. "It'll be hard with him gone. I think he'd be disappointed in the condition of things."

"No," Hack said, finally speaking up. "Blemm was never disappointed. He saw only the best in everyone." He looked up at her. "But we'd like to help you with that, maintaining the farm without him, I mean. I have some valuables that belonged to Blemm, and I know he'd want you to have them. Perhaps you can use them to hire some help. I left them in the little work shed beside the house."

Sophia nodded. "Thank you. I didn't know he had anything of much value."

Hack shrugged. "You know Blemm, always full of surprises."

"He talked about you often, Hack."

He barked a laugh. "I can just imagine."

"No, not like that," Sophia laughed. "He used to tell me there was no one on this planet smarter than Hack. Oh, he never understood all those techno gizmo things you play with, but boy, he was fascinated by *you*, no doubt."

Hack looked back at her, his own face mirroring her somber expression. "Thank you for that. He was a great man."

Sophia looked toward the front of the property. A streak of dust trailed a long white car that was approaching the house.

"This must be our other guests," Sophia said.

"Other guest?" Kalum said, but Sophia paid no attention. She turned and walked to greet the newcomers, and they all followed behind.

The limousine parked near Kalum's car and the driver came around to open the back door. Kalum smiled widely as Mariah stepped out of the car. She looked fantastic in a yellow dress and the sun reflecting her hair.

After Sophia had offered Mariah a friendly hug, Kalum stepped forward and bowed before her. "My future queen," he said.

"Stop that," Mariah admonished, but a wry grin spread over her face.

Trinn rushed forward and hugged Mariah tightly. "It's so good to see you again," she said.

Mariah smiled and eyed the still open door of the limousine. "There's someone else you'll be happy to see," she said cryptically.

They all turned as another person climbed out of the car. "Elbore," Trinn screamed and rushed to embrace him. "What in Lorr are you doing here?"

The old man smiled. "I recently return to Lorr and met with the new king. When I learned that Mariah was coming here to join you, I insisted on coming along. I very much wanted to introduce you."

Behind him, two others exited the limousine. They were an older woman, petite and lovely, and another woman, younger, but the spitting image of her mother.

"This is my wife, Shella, and my daughter, Elsa," Elbore said, smiling.

Trinn screamed in elation and hugged the old man once again.

They all made their introductions and spent the afternoon

reminiscing and remembering their friend Blemm. Elbore regaled them all with tales of his quest to Rhastor. It hadn't been easy, but after weeks of searching, he'd finally located his family in the secret care of a Rhast woman who had helped them escape their captivity. He then contacted Rothburn and made arrangements for safe travel back to Lorr.

Late in the day, as Trinn walked with Elbore and his wife about the property, and Hack entertained Sophia with tales of Blemm's heroics, Mariah sat with Kalum on the farmhouse porch.

"I can't tell you how happy I am that you and Trinn are finally together," Mariah said.

"I'm happy that it pleases you, Your Highness," Kalum quipped

Mariah rolled her eyes. "I'm never going to get used to that."

"Sure you will," Kalum said. He shook his head. "Wow. If I ever thought you'd one day be queen, I would have tried harder in our relationship."

Mariah laughed. "You needn't have tried harder," she said. "You did nothing wrong. I sometimes wish things had worked out differently, but I know deep down that it all happened the way it was supposed to. Trinn is who you were meant for. And me? I'm sure there's someone out there for me as well."

"From what I understand," Kalum said, trying to hide his grin, "there's an entire line of someones hoping to capture your heart."

Mariah laughed again. "Yes. I suppose I'll have to go through them one by one. It's my duty as princess. Ah, the rigors of royalty."

Now, Kalum laughed.

As the day grew late, and they'd all gone, Sophia walked about the farm remembering fond moments she'd spent with her husband. It was all so strange as she tried to imagine her life without him there. She made her way along the pathway that stretched around the house, and she soon found herself facing the door of the work shed.

She held her breath and mentally prepared for whatever it was of Blemm's things that Hack had left inside. It had taken her months to simply go through his few clothes and store them away. Every item, down to even an old sock, always brought a flood of tears.

She opened the door and immediately fell backward, overwhelmed by the sight. The tiny work shed was piled high, filled with gold coins. It was more gold than she'd ever seen, or even imagined. How was it possible?

Suddenly she laughed, loud and strong. "Full of surprises."

Kalum stopped the car along the side of a road overlooking the farm. Long shadows stretched over the fields as the sun settled for the day. "I'm really going to miss him," he said.

Trinn reached over and patted his leg. "We all are."

Hack was quiet, sitting in the backseat, but Kalum saw him in the mirror give Blemm a final farewell nod. Then the little man stretched his arms wide across the seat and inhaled a great breath of fresh air.

"Ahhh," he sighed deeply. "How about this weather?"